Bound for America

'*We'll soon be in America, the whole ship. Every one of us. And then nothing bad can happen any more.*'

As the great ship sailed further and further away, Ireland melted to a grey ghost on the horizon. And Kate, her stepmother, and her grandfather—all the people who had helped Eamonn through the great famine—disappeared like ghosts do when the sun comes up. Bound for America, Eamonn knew he would never see his country or his friends again. They were going to a place where land was plentiful, where there were jobs for anyone who wasn't afraid of hard work. But will the reality live up to Eamonn's dreams, or are there more hardships and heartbreaks in store for them . . . ?

ELIZABETH LUTZEIER has worked as a teacher in Germany, America, and England. She has two of her own children and 1,300 children who keep her company most days in her work as Headteacher of an 11–18 comprehensive school. Her first novel, *No Shelter*, won the Kathleen Fidler Award. Two of her books have been nominated for the Carnegie Medal and one for the Guardian Children's Fiction Award. *Bound for America* is her fourth novel for Oxford University Press and is a sequel to *The Coldest Winter*.

Bound for America

Other books by Elizabeth Lutzeier

The Coldest Winter
Crying for the Enemy

Bound for America

ELIZABETH LUTZEIER

OXFORD
UNIVERSITY PRESS

OXFORD
UNIVERSITY PRESS

Great Clarendon Street, Oxford OX2 6DP

Oxford University Press is a department of the University of Oxford.
It furthers the University's objective of excellence in research, scholarship,
and education by publishing worldwide in

Oxford New York

Auckland Cape Town Dar es Salaam Hong Kong Karachi
Kuala Lumpur Madrid Melbourne Mexico City Nairobi
New Delhi Shanghai Taipei Toronto

With offices in

Argentina Austria Brazil Chile Czech Republic France Greece
Guatemala Hungary Italy Japan Poland Portugal Singapore
South Korea Switzerland Thailand Turkey Ukraine Vietnam

Oxford is a registered trade mark of Oxford University Press
in the UK and in certain other countries

British Library Cataloguing in Publication Data available

ISBN-13: 978-0-19-275167-6
ISBN-10: 0-19-275167-0

3 5 7 9 10 8 6 4 2

Typeset by AFS Image Setters Ltd, Glasgow

Printed and bound in Great Britain by
Cox & Wyman Ltd, Reading, Berkshire

For Michael Fenn

Rise like Lions after slumber
In unvanquishable number,
Shake your chains to earth like dew
Which in sleep had fallen on you—
Ye are many—they are few.

from 'The Mask of Anarchy' by
Percy Bysshe Shelley

ONE

'The ship's lost! The ship's lost!'

Eamonn struggled to open his eyes.

'She's going down. We're all lost! Lord have mercy on our souls!'

It was a man's voice, screaming in terror. The voice was right beside Eamonn, but he couldn't open his eyes. He felt the heaving of the ship and heard objects crashing around him, far away, at the far end of the hold and then close to the berth where he slept. But he couldn't open his eyes.

'The ship's lost! The water is all to our waists!'

There was wind and sea and the howling of the wind and the breaking of the waves like cannon shot every second on the thin shell of the boat. There was a shattering and smashing as if the ship was being splintered into matchstick pieces. And there was a man screaming in the dark. Everything was dark.

Eamonn's eyes were open. He wasn't dreaming.

'The ship's lost! The Lord have mercy on our souls! The ship's lost!'

The man was screaming, and no one had shouted at him to be quiet.

From the moment Eamonn had got on board the ship with his mother and brothers, people had been shouting at babies, at mothers singing babies to sleep, at children playing—if anyone could play in that hell-hole darkness. 'Will you shut up over there and let a body get some rest?'

But no one was shouting at the screaming, sobbing man.

'The ship's lost!'

Eamonn lifted his head up. The hold was darker than

1

it had been when they first arrived inside the ship. It was night and loud and black. The waves slammed on the sides of the hold like a giant beating a drum, an angry vandal of a giant, laughing and angry and thrashing the sides of the ship to tear a hole and let in the ocean.

Bags and barrels plummeted from the top of three berths, crashing and breaking on the wooden floors. More people woke and children's cries joined the screams of the man Eamonn couldn't see.

'The ship's lost! Save our souls!'

Eamonn couldn't move. For two whole days and nights he had been sick, lying in the bunk he shared with Dermot, sick and tired and sad. And there were thirty more days of sickness and the smell of sickness, crowded in the hold with three hundred men and women and children. Thirty more days at least. He heard the lighter movements of people springing from the top berths and thumping the floor with bare feet. There was rushing and voices and the clear sound of a rush of water round the floor beneath their berth. But instead of fleeing from the danger he closed his eyes and wished it all to go away.

It was Dermot who pulled him out of the berth, thumped him in the back with his fists and made him sit upright again.

'Will you wake up, Eamonn? We have to go on deck. They're going to get out the boats.'

The ship reeled and then there was more screaming, women and men and children screaming. In among all the sound of wind and waves and crashing wood and bending of masts and metal, there was cursing and screaming as men and women fought to get close to the narrow stairs and passageways that could take them up on deck.

Eamonn and his mother, his brothers Shaun and Dermot, were at the far end of the hold, furthest away from the only escape route. Fear held Eamonn tightly from behind, fear like a tall, strong, quiet stranger, with both hands firmly pressed upon his shoulders. Eamonn's mother stood beside him, with Shaun's hand in hers. Eamonn couldn't see them in the blackness, but he could feel they were there, waiting for the crush of people to move. The icy water swept around their feet but no further. Out of the blackness he suddenly saw the moonlike white of an old face. Julia Kelly sat upright in her berth and waited.

'They should be baling out where the water's coming in,' she said. 'And it's not coming in down here. I can hear it's not down here. Here is no more water than we've had since we set sail. They should be working to bale her out, not running away.' She stayed in her berth and refused to move.

But woken up out of the nightmare, Eamonn wanted air and the wind on his face. He took his mother's other hand and pulled her away from their berth towards the still struggling mass of people crowded around the stairway. He pushed his mother up first and his brothers and gasped for the cool, fresh air that rushed at him down from the deck.

There was light on the deck, a five o'clock sunrise, warming the masses of people, huddled and wet, with wild, filthy faces and clothes torn from pulling and crushing against each other to get on deck. Light flashed out, from the waves as well as the waking-up sun. The wind had roughed up the waves to a whirl of rushing white foam, exploding and showering millions of stars against the sides of the ship. Everything moved. The ship and the sea and the sky heaved and rolled around them and the sailors screamed warnings to keep away from the railings.

Something was happening down below in the hold, but Eamonn wasn't part of it, sick again and lying flat on the freezing wet, rain-soaked, wave-soaked deck. Sailors and anyone else who could be beaten and forced to go back down below worked for hours to bale the ship out and block up the small crack made in the ship's side.

Eamonn wanted to be part of the work. Voices rang inside his head, Kate's voice, her mother's quiet looks of disapproval, Kate's grandfather urging him on. 'You've come too far to give up now, laddy.' The voices of all the people back in Ireland told him to get up off the deck, to stop the ship sinking.

But all he could do was heave himself up to sit in the row where Dermot and Mammy and Shaun had kept him a space against one of the upper deck rails. Like an old, sick man in a wheelchair, there was nothing he could do except sit and watch helplessly as the ship was thrown about by the wild wind and the waves.

Barrels and boxes struggled and tried to fly over the side at every heave and lurch of the ship. They should have been safely stowed below, but people had dragged them up on deck in the panic when they thought the ship was going down—as if they could have survived the raging sea with a chest of ragged clothing and cooking pots strapped to their backs. Somebody said a whole family with ten children had been swept overboard, a family that had camped out on the deck with only a canopy over their heads. Eamonn knew nothing about that. No one had written down their names. He wondered if anyone knew how many people had found a place to sleep in the hold of the great ship and round her decks. They had had tickets with numbers on them, but other families had come along later, with the same tickets and the same numbers. And then sailors had kicked the newcomers, the ones who had come last onto the ship, and made them move away, out of the hold and onto the deck.

So it might have been true what they said about a family of ten being swept overboard in the storm. A huge wave, people said, in the storm just before dawn, had thrown itself on them and sucked them into the water. Nobody knew who they were or where they came from, and only a few people said they had seen them. So it

4

might have been true, or it might have been part of the terrible nightmares brought by the storm. If a whole family had gone, that meant there was no one left who would miss them, no one to know they had ever set sail on the ship from Ireland.

Then the sea became quiet. With their backs to the deck-rail leading to a look-out point, Eamonn and his mother heard a worn-out sailor giving his report to the master. He said there was still water down below, but no more was coming in and the ship would be fine till she got into port. Then he laughed.

'There's an old woman still asleep, in a berth at the far end of the hold, with her arms still cradled round a ham. Anyone could have stolen it.'

Eamonn didn't want to go down into the hold again. Even when Dermot went off to check on their berths and see what had happened to the old woman, Julia Kelly, Eamonn sat and stared at the wide open picture of sky and sea. He was a fighter, his father had always said, but here there was nothing to fight. Behind them and above them on the bridge, there were two sailors still insisting that a family, with ten or twelve children, they couldn't be sure, had rigged up a canopy next to the deck-rail and had slept under there for two nights since the ship set sail. They pointed to strands of frayed rope still tugged at by the wind, where they said the canopy had been, but the captain pointed to frayed rope all around the rails. He wouldn't listen.

'That would give us more passengers than I'm licensed to carry. I know nothing about any other passengers. You know I've never carried too many. And we've never had more than the odd one or two men overboard. It's more than my licence is worth.'

Eamonn tried to picture the family they said had been lost. He tried to see them sitting on the deck, the children playing, the father with his shirt sleeves rolled up, smoking a pipe and staring at the waves. He tried to see them clinging to each other through the storm until there was nothing more for them to cling to. But he could see nothing. He had hardly been on deck the whole of the time since they had left Ireland. All he could see was the deep, grey sea and the grey, cold sky.

He didn't want to think about whole families being destroyed. He had left that behind him in Ireland, left it behind him for good. All Eamonn wanted was to be in America. There was no going back to Ireland and the house they had had in the west. There was only America, with land enough and work enough for anyone who wasn't afraid of hard work. He had thirty more days to get through, perhaps thirty-five. After that, he would never need to go to sea again.

Then late in the day, with the storm behind them, someone shouted out, 'Land! There's land ahead!' And the crowds up on deck rushed to the other side of the ship crying and laughing that they had reached America. Eamonn stood up. Mammy stood up and shook out her damp skirt and her apron, smiling.

'Now who said it was a terrible, awful journey? Look, we're nearly there, and only one bad storm. Look, Eamonn, that must be America. It's no different to any other place, if you're talking about the rain and the wind now, is it?'

She chattered on, and Eamonn watched as the faint line of land became a broad band and broke the heaving of the sea and sky.

'That's not America. It can't be.'

The damaged steamship limped up the estuary into Liverpool.

TWO

Some of the passengers were still not sure where they were as the ship edged into dock. The sailors laughed when they heard the old Irish women talking.

'Liverpool. Now isn't that part of Boston?'

Eamonn tried to ask one of the sailors.

'I thought we were going straight to America. We're going to Boston.'

'Not for a guinea, you isn't. Anyway, this wreck couldn't have got us safe to Boston. You'll need to book your passage through to Boston now and then wait for a ship. I hope you've got your money ready.'

Eamonn lied. He had heard of the thieving at Liverpool, the runners who carried your bags for you and then ran away and you never saw them again. 'That was all the money we had. I'll have to find work before we can sail again.'

Old Julia Kelly was standing beside them.

'You stick to me and I can help with your passage,' she said. 'And then you can pay me back when we get to Boston. There's more work there, and good money to be earned, they say. I'm going out to join my daughter.'

Eamonn wanted to shut her up with her talk about having money to spare, but he was too late. The tall sailor hovered close by, picking up her bag and carrying it down the gangplank for her. Eamonn turned back to carry the bundle his mother had brought, a blanket each and their Sunday clothes. Then he took Shaun by the hand and looked for Julia Kelly in the crowd on the quay. But the old woman was gone.

The sailor they had spoken to was standing just beside the gangplank and signing to some men below. If he tapped his nose with his finger, one of the men from the crowd round the gangplank grabbed hold of a passenger's bags as soon as they left the ship and shot away, smiling, with the passenger running after him. When it was their turn to leave the ship, Eamonn saw the sailor making his thumb and first finger into a nought, and none of the men came near them.

Then an older man strolled up, yawning. 'Passages arranged. Nothing but the best. Will you be wanting a bed for the night?' He wiped a tar-stained sleeve on his mud-stained face.

Eamonn refused any help. He had no idea what anything cost. His mother had stitched the bag with their money into one of her wide skirts. With the money left over from paying their fares he had hoped to buy food and land. Now he wasn't even sure if what he had would give them their fare to America. He wasn't going to waste it on seeing the sights of Liverpool. His mother looked to him now as head of the family and he needed time to think.

They had to find a good, safe ship at a price they could afford. They had to get away quickly, before their money ran out. The storms of the night before had given way to sweltering heat in the grand, filthy city of Liverpool. It was the beginning of August. A boy showed them the way to Goree Piazza and they walked up and down the hot, dusty road, examining all the posters with pictures of ships, the prices next to each journey and the number of tons the ship was.

'How do we know what's a good one?'

Dermot had taken to whispering from the moment they arrived in the great, bustling city. He held tight to his mother's hand, something he hadn't done for a year or two. If they stopped for a minute to look in a ship-broker's window, boys and men crowded around them.

'Irish are you? Do you want the best passage out? Very safe?'

'Let Murphy's of Liverpool fix you up with a place to stay.'

Mammy pulled at the three of them. 'Come away. They'll not leave us alone around here.' They moved on to Waterloo Road, where the American packet ships lay.

'There are no ships with steam,' Shaun said. 'Only the sail ships.'

'Shush!' Mammy did not want the men and boys who surrounded them near every ship's office to hear their Irish accents. But their clothes gave them away, their worn, clean clothes. And their small bundle of belongings told the whole city they were emigrants, people just dying to hand over their money to anyone clever enough to get it out of them.

After they had walked the whole length of both streets crowded with shipping agents and food shops, Shaun said, 'I counted twenty public houses all in that street. Can anyone go in?' They had never seen such wealth, so many people, so much of everything.

'They shouldn't have beggars in a city as grand as this,' Mammy said. She would have given away half their money to the men and boys and even little, dirty scrawny girls with signs which read, 'My children are dying of hunger. Please have mercy on my little Florence and give her a penny.' But Eamonn tugged at her skirts, checking at every street crossing that the bag of coins was still there, stitched and fixed securely to the lining.

At least now they knew what they'd have to pay. Though the men chasing after them had offered them tickets for anything from £1 to £10, a lot of the signs in windows said £3 10s. Dermot and Shaun would each count as half a passenger and pay half the price. They were used to sharing a bed. In a quiet lane, they took the money out and counted it. When the ten guineas was gone, they would only have £7 left to start their new life.

'But we'll find ourselves some work,' Mammy said. 'And your father's sister will help us, if we only can get ourselves over there.'

They chose a ship called *The Sisters* because a broker pointed out the captain to them, and Mammy said he looked kind. Their ship was due to set sail at afternoon tide on the 4th August.

It was late afternoon and still the runners wouldn't leave them alone, even after they had paid their passage and left the broker's office.

'Nice lodging house? Cheap and respectable.'

On their long road to Tullamore, they had slept outside in the hedges and under the stars, and certainly the weather was fit for sleeping outside if you had little money and needed to save the bit you had. But Eamonn decided they had to have shelter against the clouds of runners who descended on them at every corner, like mosquitoes after rain.

The lodging house they chose, quite by accident, was paradise. First they had followed a man who wanted to show them a place to sleep to a dark, stinking cellar where the man told them there were too many thieves about in Liverpool and offered to look after all their money. Even Shaun knew that was a trick they had best keep well away from. So they set off back to the street where their ship's broker had been, to ask his advice.

Halfway there, they stopped to look at a beautiful masted sailing ship in Clarence Dock; Mammy got talking to a woman standing at the doorway of a warehouse. She told them the good places as well as the ones where they'd rip the shoes off your feet and soon they were settled in the finest lodging house at 4*d* per person per night. There was no food to be had there, but there were proper beds and sheets and they could wash themselves in cold water. The woman at the front desk even asked if they wanted writing paper.

Eamonn started to write a letter to Kate, but it was

hard to know what to say. He wanted to write good news, knowing the bad news they had every day in Ireland. So he wrote about how well they'd come out of the crush as they boarded the ship, and then left that to tell her another time. Then he wrote about the ship sailing so far off course that it took them two days to reach Liverpool, but he left that alone as well. Then he made himself write about the night of the terrible storm and how they felt themselves lucky to be alive, and the family of ten children that might have been there and might have got themselves killed. But Kate wouldn't want to read all that. She'd want to read about the good things that were going to happen to them when they got to America. It felt ungrateful to write and tell Kate about terrible hardships on the way, after all she had done, and all the money she'd given them. So Eamonn decided to leave his writings until they got to America.

Their ship did not sail the next day. Another ship took to the tide before them and, ten minutes down the estuary, started to burn, with the flames chasing each other from end to end of the vessel. Nobody knew how the fire started. They said a passenger might have been smoking down below in the hold. Or perhaps a sailor searching for stowaways had dropped his candle. Nobody knew anything about it, except that nearly four hundred were crying on the decks, screaming to be rescued, and leaping into the water when they couldn't swim.

All the first class cabin passengers were saved. Other passengers turned up, wet but unharmed, dragged out of the River Mersey by all the small boats and barges that rushed to help. No one could say if anyone was killed.

But for two whole days, no ships set sail. Eamonn and Dermot walked down to the river at dusk, where the smell of the burning vessel still hung in the air and scavengers combed the mud for anything worth money that had escaped the fire.

Dermot said, 'Shall we not go back to Ireland?'

'We would have to go on a ship to go back to Ireland. And ships can sink as well as burn.'

'But, Eamonn, if we go back to Ireland, we'll only be on a ship for a day or two.'

'There's no work for us back in Ireland. There's nothing there.'

Eamonn glared at the churned up brown-grey waters of the Mersey. Stripes of yellow foam rolled in on the tide and then stuck to the mud. There was no way out. Grandma, his father, his baby sister, all had been taken by disease and hunger when all they wanted was to find a job and just enough food to eat. There was no going back to Ireland.

'But, Eamonn, Kate's grandad will look after us. He won't let us die. We can work for him.'

'He has no work. And I won't be a beggar. Daddy never wanted us to be beggars. In America, there's work and land for anyone who's not afraid of work.'

Dermot stopped and picked up stones and pitched them one by one at the water, but none of them bounced. All of them sank beneath the murky grey-brown.

'But what will happen to us all, on a ship like that one yesterday, Eamonn? Eamonn, I'm scared. I'm scared we'll all be drowned. Or burned to death. And Mammy's scared though she won't tell you. Let's go back to Ireland, Eamonn.'

'We're bound for America.'

Their ship was larger than any they had seen so far. *The Sisters* wasn't a steam ship, so no smoke clouded the quay where they waited to embark the next day early. Instead, crowds of runners tried to separate them, from each other, from their bundles, from their money. But they held close together, Eamonn carrying Shaun on his shoulders, and watched as sailors rolled barrels and heaved huge, heavy boxes up the gangplanks. The sails, what they could see of them, looked white and bright, not ragged or dirty. More and more passengers arrived, with saucepans and hams on their shoulders or elegant boxes and trunks that gave nothing away about what was inside.

Dermot and Mammy pointed to a family, a row of sons all dressed up in top hats and tailored suits, a row of five daughters in dresses that looked like silk.

'They'll be for the cabins.'

Dermot was making himself an expert on ships.

'The money it must cost!' Mammy clutched their bundle of blankets with both hands. 'To have cabins for all of them.' Then she smiled at Eamonn. 'America must be a grand place if there's room for all these people.'

The cabin people went on first and then lined the deck-rails watching while the other passengers struggled to board. Before the steerage passengers got near the gangplank a long table was set up, and sailors started to herd the people into long lines.

A priest was first behind the table, with his white cassock.

'Are you Catholic?' he whispered, as each group of passengers approached. Eamonn, from a long way back in the line, heard him pronounce a blessing over and over again: 'From all the perils of the sea, may the good Lord bless you and preserve you.' As he got closer he saw people slip a coin into the priest's hand before they were passed on to the next man in line behind the table. One or two people shook their heads when he whispered, 'Are you Catholic?' and they set off on the journey without a blessing.

Eamonn wanted to joke with Dermot. Where were the priests from the Church of England? Were all the Protestants meant to drown? He wanted to say, 'You'll be all right now, Dermot. Now we've had a blessing, nothing can happen to us.' He wanted to laugh and cry. He thought of the people in the burning ship and wondered if they'd had a blessing before they went on their way.

Mammy smiled. 'I call that very nice and thoughtful of the priest, to come along here and bless our ship.'

Eamonn was glad their money was so safely stowed away that Mammy couldn't reach it and give some to the priest. He had already collected more than enough from the poor people.

There were two doctors next in line on the long table. Eamonn didn't realize what the two men were doing there until he was past the priest and his mother was next in line. He had never been near a doctor in his life, unless you counted the young doctor who had looked after his father and all the others in the fever tents in Tullamore. Some folk said their doctor had died from overwork, from working day and night for all the weeks the fever raged, trying to save the people. Others said he had died of a broken heart, from watching all the other people die, the sick and starving people he couldn't help. But he probably just caught the fever like all the rest of them. The fever had carried off Eamonn's father, even though he was a fighter. And the doctor had been young and pale and sad, always with sick people, never with people like Eamonn who had no sign of the sickness on them.

Eamonn was worried about his mother. The doctors would get to her next, and she wasn't strong. Maybe they should have stayed another week on land, trying to get some food inside them, with the money Kate had given them, getting their strength back. Mammy was weak and pale from a year or more of struggling to find food or work and from watching in the fever tents while Eamonn's father died. What if it turned out she had taken the fever as well? He had heard people say that a doctor could tell everything about you, that they could see right into your insides and know everything that was wrong with you. What would happen if the doctors turned them away and wouldn't let them on the ship because Mammy was sickening with the fever?

But Mammy and Shaun had passed by the doctors

already and now they were asking Eamonn, both doctors firing quick questions at him that he scarcely had time to answer.

'What's your name? Good.'

'Are you well? Right.'

'Hold out your tongue. All right.'

'Next person.'

They waited for Dermot and then, clinging to each other, made their way for the second time up the gangplank ready to set off for America.

'Isn't this a grand boat, the nicest of all, don't you think?' Mammy looked around, excited. If she had any doubts about the journey, she kept them to herself. And Eamonn too felt good about the ship they had chosen to sail on. *The Sisters* was a fine, tall ship and he overheard two men, rich and elegant in their top hats and morning coats talking to one of the officers.

'How long will she take to get to Boston?'

'The captain drives her faster every time. There's nothing this ship can't do. She's not as fast as the steamships, mind, but a deal more comfortable. With a good wind, we can make Boston in thirty days.'

'Did you hear that, Eamonn?' Dermot grabbed at his elbow while they were walking past the men and making their way to the steep stairs that led below deck. Then he turned round and walked backwards, trying to hear more of their conversation and feasting his eyes on their fine clothes.

'We are going to land in America on the third of September.'

They didn't stay down in the hold for long. *The Sisters* had open shafts that let in chinks of light and air to the passengers piled in below deck in steerage, but still it was better to be up above as the graceful ship slid slowly out of the dock and into the wide, crowded river.

Rowing boats and larger tugs, flat-bottomed barges and fishing vessels all looked in danger of being knocked away by the huge sailing boat, but they all managed to slip off to the side just in time as *The Sisters* made her way downstream. Eamonn started to look at their fellow-passengers as the city of Liverpool fell back, further and further away from them.

'Buy us some of these, Eamonn. I just had some juice. Buy us some oranges.'

The orange-sellers were two young women with bare feet and skirts hitched up above their ankles. All they had with them were baskets of oranges, nothing else for the voyage. There were other people with things to sell. One man carried a suitcase full of maps of America. He said you couldn't move in America without a map and a crowd of passengers stood round him as he pointed out parts of the country coloured in pink and green and talked of rattlesnakes and swamps, orchards and cotton fields. Another man went round to the gentlemen in top hats, asking them all if they had bought their sun hats for the tropical weather conditions. Some of them laughed at him. Others gave him money and took in return a white hat like a soldier's helmet.

It was like being at a fair. Then a cannon boomed and the ship slowed down almost to a standstill as a large rowing boat, rowed by eight bare-chested men, came up alongside. A group of drunken men scrambled, laughing, out of the boat and onto the rope ladder that hung down the side of the ship. Passengers leaned over the side, all laughing as well, while the final, drunken sailors pretended to fall into the water and performed all the acrobatic tricks they could manage after two days of drinking before they crawled on board and joined the rest of the crew.

Then the orange-sellers and the hat man, the map man, and a man who had sold all his supply of snake-bite medicine first threw their baskets and boxes and then followed after them, down the rope ladder and into the rowing boat. The passengers gave a cheer as the rowing boat cast off and the great sailing ship finally shook off the crowd of followers that had clung on and been pulled along in her wake all the way from Waterloo Dock.

They had a good, strong ship and a crew who would sober up in an hour or two. They had a captain who was famous for taking care of his passengers and getting them safely into port.

Ahead of them lay the open sea, and in thirty days, America.

THREE

Their ship, *The Sisters*, was a wonderful adventure, a Promised Land, a place where everyone, rich and poor, was made to feel important. From the moment they lost sight of land, the people on board behaved differently. It was just as if they were already Americans, sharing their lives together in their new country. Even the first-class passengers, the ones with cabins up high near where the captain had his quarters, the families dressed up in silk who ate dinner with Captain Christian every evening, were not too proud to go between the decks.

'And why should they be proud?' Mammy put her best dress on one night when someone brought out a fiddle and a whistle and people were dancing in the space cleared of boxes. Everyone knew that in America all of the people were treated the same, rich or poor.

'And we'll soon be rich when we get there,' people said. They danced under the stars until the whistle blew for twelve o'clock. And the rich people, standing round after dinner in their silks and evening suits, clapped their hands and swayed to the music. The very large family all with their cabins and their servants used to come as well and a line of the daughters in almost identical dresses stood in front of the sons, all eager to enjoy the party. At the end of each dance they clapped politely and were chaperoned off to bed at ten o'clock.

'They'll stay longer tomorrow,' the fiddle player said. 'And we'll have them dancing too before the journey's over.'

There was a family of English actors on board as well as all the Irish with their fiddles and whistles. The actors called themselves the Leopardis, even though their proper name was Taylor and they said they were practising to put on a show the very minute the ship arrived in Boston. There wasn't space enough for them to practise on the narrow decks where the cabins were, so they were down between decks every day, with crowds of passengers watching while their two young sons and their tiny daughter tumbled backwards and forwards all over the deck.

Dermot said Mrs Leopardi looked far too miserable for an actress, but Eamonn said that was because she played the sad parts. He said she had had to practise being sad so much she had probably forgotten how to be happy.

They were never seasick in the early days of the journey. Eamonn had pushed from his mind the memory of the terrible journey over the Irish sea when every movement made him sick. He found himself laughing at how afraid they had been about the journey and pleased that he had kept his fears to himself when all the rest of the family had wanted to go back to Ireland. They didn't have much food, less than most other families, but what they had was more than they had managed on for weeks when the potatoes had failed in the west of Ireland.

They were having a wonderful time. Every evening, the cabin passengers became a little braver, until one night the liveliest girl from the very large family started to twirl round in time to the music, holding her brother's hand. There was clapping and cheering and the Leopardis all joined in, turning the jig into a tremendous display of tumbling. After that, a message went round that the steerage passengers would be allowed to use the walkways round the decks where the cabins were, as long as they behaved themselves, instead of having to climb down into the deep, dark hold to get from one end of the ship to another.

Everyone was smiling and relaxed. Whatever class they were travelling people greeted each other in the morning and the evening. Eamonn felt they were among friends.

Then the water shortage began.

At first, people said that some of the barrels had leaked. It was no one's fault. They would all just have to be a little more careful. The ladies in first class didn't appear so often.

'Don't want to get themselves dirty,' one of the mates said, 'when there ain't no water to wash with.'

They were forbidden to use anything except sea water to wash themselves.

One day, the rumour went round that there was going to be coffee handed out to everyone at the end of the day.

'What's coffee?'

'Don't know. But you can drink it. Americans drink coffee.'

The coffee tasted of bitter salt water. Eamonn drank one cup and then rushed to the side of the boat to spit out whatever he had left in his mouth, gasping for a cup of fresh water to take away the taste.

A lot of the passengers threw their hard, salt biscuits overboard too. They had their own provisions with them. But Dermot and Eamonn did their best, gnawing at the hard biscuits as if they were some kind of sweet.

The decks emptied. The sun was burning in spite of the cool breeze from the ocean and people were too tired to dance. At night, the fiddlers still played between decks, but the Leopardis had stopped their tumbling. Eamonn was worried. Mammy started to lie down all day in her berth in the crowded hold because she said the thirst didn't get to her so much that way. Shaun was quiet, and sat in the shade on deck, with his back to the wall of one of the first class cabins.

Eamonn had days where he hung his head right over the side of the ship, his stomach heaving from being sick. His head, heavy, felt as if it were falling away from him. He only had to let go of the rail to follow the weight of his head, hanging, falling into the waves.

It wasn't seasickness. The waves were calm. And anyway, they'd been out at sea long enough to get used to the wildest storm. All they were given to eat were hard, salt biscuits, hard because they had been stored for months and specially hardened so they wouldn't go mouldy. There wasn't enough water and the salt of the biscuits dried your mouth and made your stomach churn.

Nobody could say whose fault it was. They had started out with barrels of water enough. Then the water in some of the barrels had started to froth and swim with insects and scum and one of the sailors had thrown it all overboard. They thought the infection, the scum and the dirt, would spread to all the barrels.

So they each got a cup of water, once a day, standing in long lines to get their water and salt biscuit. And there were still fifteen more days to go if they kept on course.

The decks emptied. More than four hundred people disappeared. In the deep, dark hold where the steerage berths were piled three high and the space between each berth was no bigger than a baby could lie down in, people lay in their beds, too weary to move. It was quiet in the hold, hot and full of sickness and quiet.

Eamonn made Dermot walk with him round the decks every morning and they both helped Mammy and Shaun to go round the ship once every evening after it got dark. He wasn't going to let them give up. He gritted his teeth every morning when all he wanted to do was to carry on sleeping, in spite of the sickening, thick dark smells that surrounded him like a fog. They had to keep moving. He wasn't going to get them this far only to die out at sea for a cup of water. Every day he counted the days backwards. Only ten more days to go.

He repeated the words to anyone he saw, men and women who had been dancing and laughing only a week before.

'Only ten more days to go.'

But there was no answer.

He repeated the words like a charm, as if saying them would make them come true.

'Only ten more days to go.'

Up on deck, in the evenings, they saw bright lights in the captain's cabin, soft lights in the other cabins along the way.

'They probably have a drop more water,' Mammy whispered. 'It's only right. They'll have paid a good deal more to sail.'

One night they heard a young girl's voice crying out, 'Water! For pity's sake, water!' And they held close to the outside wall of the cabin and heard a gentle voice saying, 'Damp her head with this cloth. Cool her down with the sea water at least.' All along the top deck, they could still hear the young girl's voice crying out for water.

Mammy shook her head. 'That's the fever,' she said. 'The fever that took your daddy. It's the fever that's talking, even if she had all the water in the world.'

After that night, the passengers in steerage weren't allowed to walk along the first class deck. Their only chance to get a look at the sea was to walk right through from one end of the dark, stinking hold to the other and climb the steps at the far end. Eamonn made them all walk up on deck once a day at least.

For the first two weeks of travel they had scrubbed the ship, all of the decks every day. People had jumped and laughed as they dodged the buckets of dirty, dusty water slopped around the floor by sailors who knew they would be in trouble if the people in the hold were left to sink in their own dirt.

But suddenly there were not enough sailors left to muck out the hold. And the ones who were left didn't want to go down where the air had started to smell of death and sickness.

A farmer's wife from the country near Cork was the first to die down in the hold. They heard her too, crying out for water, when everyone in the hold had learned to manage on half a cup of water a day. Then the silence in the hold was broken by her merry voice, first laughing and saying, 'There's nothing wrong with me that a touch of dry land won't put right,' and then shouting, 'Why are you making me keep to my bed in this mess and this stinking hole? There's nothing wrong with me, I say. I have to be up and milking.'

It was getting towards night and Eamonn wanted to make sure they got to look at the sea again, just to see how close they were to America. Maybe they could already see land from the ship. 'Only eight more days to go,' he said to Mammy, standing up straight while she leaned heavily on him and made herself walk. 'We should be seeing land soon.'

They reached the far end of the hold, where the farmer from Cork had his berth, the place where the shouting had come in the afternoon. Now everything was quiet.

'She's sleeping.' The farmer glanced up at them as they went past. 'I think she'll do all right now the worst is over.'

Mammy waited until they were up on deck. 'She'll be gone before morning,' she said, 'and soon we'll all be gone.'

Eamonn pulled her away from the stairs. 'Come on out of that. We'll soon be in America, the whole ship. Every one of us. And then nothing bad can happen any more.'

There was a loud cry, coming from down below. Mammy turned round, hugging Shaun to her, and looked towards the hatch they had just climbed out of. Two sailors moved towards the hatch and then stood at the opening, waiting.

Someone was crying, someone climbing slowly up the stairs they had just climbed, and crying like a child with a loud, man's voice. Then he started to shout, first angry shouting, then sobbing like a lost child. 'They've killed her at last. I tried to stop them. I brought her away from all that hunger and sickness back home. But they've killed her at last.' The farmer climbed up to the last rickety step, a big, strong man weeping like a child. He pointed down into the hold.

'Go down and look at her, will you. Look at the way they've killed her.'

Mammy let go of Shaun, pushing him off to Dermot, and caught hold of the man's arm.

'The sailors didn't kill her.' Mammy put her arm around the man's shoulder. 'The water wasn't their fault. There was nothing they could do.'

'I never said the sailors killed her.' The man pressed both his fists over his eyes and then turned away from them. 'The landlord murdered her at last,' he said, 'the English murderer who threw us off our land and left us with nowhere else to go.'

They said prayers that night, with the body sewn into a shroud, and then threw the woman overboard.

After that, the captain came down into the hold every day. Any passengers who could still walk around helped to scrub the decks and make them as clean as they could.

'Five more days to Boston, is it?' Eamonn stood close to the captain one day when he entered the hold to watch over the cleaning out.

'I'm afraid it may take longer than five days.' The captain's glance took in the high, packed berths, with people weak from fever and thirst. 'And if the fever means Boston won't take us, we may have to head for Canada.'

Another ten days passed. Eamonn had watched and waited for land for too long, peering through the captain's eyeglass, willing his family to survive. When he saw the thin line that was the land along the St Lawrence estuary, he went off to the far side of the empty deck, put his head in his hands and cried. His mother and both his brothers were alive and free of the fever as far as anyone could be free of it, living with the smell of it for nearly a month.

He had convinced himself that as soon as they touched land nothing bad would happen any more.

Eamonn looked up and stared at the thin dark line on the horizon, ashamed of himself for being so pleased that his family were still alive. He had no idea who else had survived the catastrophe. The cabin passengers should have been crowding the deck-rails now that the sailors had started the cry, 'Land ahoy!' But the deck remained empty. It started to get dark, the land got closer and Captain Christian walked past. 'We won't be landing tonight, young man. They'll want to look at the sick on board.'

Still Eamonn stood there, with his chin down on his hands, staring at the place in the dark sky where he knew the land must be.

His mother came up behind him, holding the others by the hand.

'Where's the land, Eamonn? Where's America?'

Eamonn turned round and grinned. 'It's not America. It's Canada. But that doesn't matter. We're here, Mammy. We've arrived.'

'Would you look at that beautiful sky!' Mammy said. 'Did you ever see anything so beautiful before? Even the moon looks larger.'

FOUR

'Are you a plague ship? Do you have the fever on board?'

In late September 1847, after fifty days at sea, Captain Christian steered his ship to anchor off Grosse Isle, just outside Quebec. There were eight seamen left and none of them would help him with the terrible job of bringing the dead out of the hold. The captain had promised that passengers who died in sight of land should be buried on dry land. So he brought them out of the hold himself, carrying them up on his strong shoulders and lining them up on the deck to be sewn into their shrouds.

'We have sick men, women, and children on board and we need water. Only send us some water.'

A long line of small boats ferried between the island and the tall ships waiting to disembark. Eamonn counted fourteen ships, all just as large, all with their cargoes of emigrants waiting to get to America. One boat brought water to their ship, and the five people who had died the night before were taken off, but all the other passengers had to stay.

More people came up on deck to stare at the land they could not touch. Exhausted, and most of them sick, they drank and then sat slumped with their backs to the side of the ship, waiting only to get on land. For a whole day they sat there, glad to be out of the stench of the hold.

Cabin passengers joined them, thin and pale. Eamonn looked for the family with five daughters and four sons, but he couldn't see them anywhere. The Leopardi family were all there, but none of them tumbled or sang.

The ship was full of ghosts.

Eamonn's mother whispered, 'What are we waiting for? Why are they keeping us from shore?'

Eamonn swept his arm around, pointing to the fourteen other ships at anchor. 'They're all waiting. A doctor has to come and look at them, to see if they've got fever.'

'We have got fever.' Dermot stared at Eamonn as if he was stupid. 'That's why we need to get away from here. There's too much fever.'

'Why don't they send a doctor?' A man from the cabins, a man they had not seen since they set off from Liverpool, joined the small circle of people gathering round Eamonn and his family.

Eamonn shrugged his shoulders. Why did they think he knew all the answers? He was thirteen. All he had done was to help the captain when everyone else was too sick or too keen on saving their own necks. All he knew was what Captain Christian had told him when they walked the hold together at night, looking after the very sick passengers.

'They don't want the fever to come into Canada from any of these ships. So they make people stay in quarantine. On that island.'

'Well, why don't they put us on the island, and get on with it?'

The man sounded like someone who was used to telling people what to do.

Eamonn frowned. 'A doctor has to check the ships first and see how bad things are.'

'Well, where is the doctor? Hmm?'

Eamonn stood up and once again swept with his arm over the horizon, pointing out each of the fourteen other ships.

'They were all here before us.'

'Are they just going to leave us all here to die?'

'We have food and water now.'

'Aye, food and water and the fever.' The man had tears in his eyes. 'My brother is waiting for me in Boston.'

Captain Christian walked past them on the upper deck. He looked tired.

'What's all this, sir?'

The man from the cabins had on a long, green frock coat and shoes that shone like new oil paint.

'Mr Froggat? How can I help you? Good to see you taking the air again, sir.'

'Enough of that, man. I've paid well for this voyage, but I'm prepared to pay more. What will it cost to take me off in one of those small boats there? I am expected in Boston. They can't expect me to stay here with these people.'

'I cannot do it for a thousand pounds, sir.'

The crowd around the captain grew larger. Passengers who had been too tired to walk around stood up and crowded round to listen.

'My servant is sick. He needs a doctor.'

'We have thirty people on board who need the doctor, sir. And he will come, when he can come. They say he works night and day and still the ships come, loaded with their poor and sick people.'

'Why aren't there more doctors? There should be two for every ship. What sort of a country is this? And why don't the poor stay at home?'

Eamonn was glad he didn't have to answer the man's questions. The way he talked made Eamonn smile and then made him sad, all in one go. The man was used to having whatever his money could buy. He had bought himself space and fresh air for the voyage, with one of the best cabins on board. He had been able to buy himself good food, fine clothes, and a manservant. But Captain Christian was not to be bought. And the fever didn't care how much money passengers had.

That night, fiddle music was played on *The Sisters* again, for the first time in a month and a small number of passengers stood around and clapped and sang, happy to be at least in sight of land.

That night, Mr Froggat's servant died, and two more passengers from the cabins. Eamonn saw the last surviving members of the large family, a sister and her brother, weeping as their mother and a sister were taken off in one of the small boats which was only used for the dead. And he was angry again, and his eyes stung as he remembered the anger that had made him scream and cry and hammer against the hard wall of the workhouse in Tullamore where his father had died of the fever. He wasn't going to lose the rest of his family, whatever happened. He was not going to let them die. He stared again towards land, willing them all to get there safely, because nothing bad could happen once they touched land in America or Canada. The country they landed in didn't matter. All that mattered was to get his family onto dry land.

Eamonn's mother and Dermot and Shaun had begun to recover from the voyage, now there was fresh water every day. They had money still, to buy food, and Dermot and Shaun chased each other round the decks. Eamonn made them stay above, made them sleep on deck to keep away from the terrible smell that wouldn't leave the hold however much they scrubbed the decks there every day.

Captain Christian, without a ship to sail, spent most of his time looking after the sick down in the hold and Eamonn wanted to help him. He had no fear for himself, as long as his family kept out of the way of the sickness.

By the fourth day, ten people had died of the fever since they had sighted land. In the evening, a doctor was piped aboard, with two assistants. Dr Douglas was his name. He went into the captain's cabin and came out looking serious.

Mr Froggat went straight up to him.

'Can I see you, Doctor Douglas, in my cabin? If we can get the formalities over I can arrange a boat and they can send my luggage later . . . '

Doctor Douglas shook his hand and then shook his

head. 'One thing at a time, sir. One thing at a time. A case like this cannot be rushed. I will come to your cabin with pleasure, sir. But first we must look in the hold.'

Eamonn went down with them. The doctors were pleased with the way they had kept the hold clean and told of the ships they had seen where no one had cleaned down below for the whole of a voyage.

But the hold was far less crowded than it had been. Eamonn had not stood before and had a proper look around the hold. He had no idea how many passengers had joined the ship at Liverpool. All he knew was that every berth had been full when they set sail. Now, the hold was quiet and calm and everywhere there were gaps, where people used to be. He had known about every one of the deaths as they happened, one by one, but he had never before looked at the whole catastrophe. How could he not have noticed so many people disappearing?

'Anyone lost overboard? Natural causes?'

'One eighty-year-old woman, just off the coast of Ireland.'

Doctor Douglas was running his finger down a list of names. Eamonn could see that some of them were only half-names. 'Kelly family one . . . Kelly family two . . . Kelly family three . . . ' Did no one know their names? At first, he thought the long list had the names of all the passengers who had set sail—though no one had asked for their names when they went on board or when they bought their tickets. Then he realized that the long, long list held names of all the people who had died, of typhoid fever, on board ship.

'We'll have to distribute people before they go on land,' the doctor said. 'Some to the hospital, some to the fever sheds. If we are lucky we can send most to the quarantine tents. Shall we start making a record now?'

The doctors seemed to know which patients couldn't last much longer. Even Eamonn had seen enough to recognize the time when fever patients seemed to be getting better, just before the crisis when they died. The worst patients were sent to the fever sheds. The ones they thought might pull through were marked out for the hospital, as long as there were beds for them. If there was no more room, the people would have to be put in tents. And Doctor Douglas said he never knew when there would be room again, there were so many ships arriving with cargoes of sick people.

In the midst of all that horror, there was good news. Eamonn and his mother and brothers were told they only had to stay in the quarantine tents for a while to make sure they were clear of the sickness.

They were among the last to leave the ship, climbing into the small boat that carried Captain Christian and the first mate. Behind them was Ireland and hunger, the ship and the fever. Ahead of them they could see Grosse Isle, great grey rocks and a blue sky, and woods with trees just beginning to turn red and orange and brown. A smile went round the boat like a flash of lightning, striking everyone who sat there.

'How far is it from Canada to Boston?' Dermot asked. 'Will we get there by Sunday?'

FIVE

Nothing mattered, now that they had landed in Canada. They had to sleep on the ground because there were no beds, but they slept well. The tents kept falling down, because no one had been able to pitch the extra army tents properly on ground where the rocks were only a few inches below the surface. But Eamonn and his family laughed at the tents. They had had to sleep outside in the fiercest weather in Ireland, and they knew that the quarantine was not forever.

Their tent was only one of hundreds in long rows all along the base of a hill, with a gap of at least fifty yards between the highest row of tents and the fever sheds.

'There's no need to be afraid down here. Captain Christian told me the gap is wide enough to keep the fever out.'

The captain had been in and out of the fever sheds and the hospital, visiting the sick from his ship and helping to care for the ones who needed help. There was only one doctor on the island and five or six nurses for hundreds of fever cases.

Eamonn could see his mother and brothers getting better every day. His brothers dodged around and ran among the tents, forgetting where they were. He had to shout at them to make them keep away from the fever sheds. His mother went out for long walks, which pleased him until he found out that she was visiting the sick people she had got to know on the boat.

'The doctor is such a good man,' she said, 'but he is more than likely going to drop dead with the work he does here. Like our good captain, he never stops.' She smiled. 'I never knew there were so many good people in the world, Eamonn.'

Eamonn didn't want to be good. He wanted to get them away from the island as soon as possible. The fever was a beast with its jaws wide open, waiting to devour them.

The captain asked Eamonn's mother to look after Mr Froggat, the rich man who had tried to pay to leave quarantine. She stayed with him in the hospital until he died, holding his hand while he shouted at her and told her he could pay for a proper doctor if only she would stop being so stupid and go and get him one.

After Mr Froggat died, she said, 'I wish I could write, Eamonn. Maybe you can write for me. Someone ought to write and tell his poor family that he had a peaceful death.'

Eamonn turned and walked away from her. How could she stay so calm? How could she talk of a peaceful death, as if there was anything that would make people dying any better? He turned his back on her and walked right down the slope, to the edge of the cliff, where the waves carried on their hundred-thousand-year-old work of battering and biting at the land until pieces of rock fell into the sea.

On the way back to the rows of tents, struggling up the steep slope, Eamonn noticed a pipe that came out of the ground and disgorged filthy water that trickled down an open channel and out into the sea. The smell was enough to make him retch. He had to get his family away.

It had been raining heavily, the night before Dr Douglas gave them permission to go, in a steamer that would take them on to Quebec or Montreal, but Mammy refused to leave. Captain Christian had staggered into the hospital announcing he was going to set sail for Bermuda and the doctor had had to admit him too, with the typhoid fever.

'We can't leave here as long as there is no one left to help the doctor,' Mammy said. 'I have been with the fever many a time before. I'll be one of those as doesn't get fever. See if I'm not.' She pulled up her skirts as she jumped over the mud at the entrance to their tent from where it had been raining the night before. 'Only see that Dermot and Shaun keep away from the hospital.'

'And who's going to see that you keep away? What about you?' Eamonn shouted after her. Then he turned back into the tent and hit out at their wet bundle of clothes. Shaun and Dermot were outside laughing, wrestling with other boys in the muddy hole that had once been the strip of grass between the tents and the fever sheds. When it rained, the smell of the filthy water draining into the pipe just beyond their tents hung in the air and swooped around them like a great, grey-brown bat.

For days and days there was nothing for Eamonn to do, except shout at his brothers every time their feet strayed anywhere outside an invisible boundary Eamonn had shown them. His mother came back to their tent in the evenings, but he wanted to know what she was doing all day, so he followed her up to the hospital. He had never been inside and the smell made him run outside again to catch his breath.

'What's your business here, lad?' The doctor was no more tired than on all the other days he had spent being called out all night. He was no rougher or more impatient than usual. 'No one should be around here unless they've got business here. This is not a place for a healthy boy like you, laddie.'

'But you've got my mother in there!'

'I'm sorry to hear that, laddie. But it's better for you if you keep away.'

'She's not sick. She just comes in here to help. Where is she?'

They found Eamonn's mother sitting quietly in the middle of a long, quiet room, filled with fifty beds. She was holding Captain Christian's hand.

'He needs someone to talk to. To cheer him up,' she said. 'He was talking rubbish all last night. But when I got here this morning, he had his eyes wide open and a smile for me and said he felt much better.' She smiled at Eamonn. 'I think I'm doing him some good. I couldn't help poor Mr Froggat. But if I can help the captain who was so good and got us all safe here . . .'

Dr Douglas leaned over the sick man. 'It won't be long now,' was all he said and then, 'Come along, laddie, if you want to do some work for me. There's a penny or two and some bread and milk.'

Mammy refused to believe that the captain was dead. She had gone back to their tent to look to Shaun and Dermot and when she returned to the ward he was gone. She shook her head. 'He was getting better,' she said. 'And he would not have set sail without saying goodbye.'

Eamonn showed her why the captain would never set sail again, showed her the tall ship, still there in the lanes outside Grosse Isle, with not enough people to sail her. But she refused to believe him. 'I don't know what our ship looked like. What do I know about ships? He was getting better. Anyone could see that. So where has he gone to?'

Eamonn took her to the mound of newly dug graves, not near the church, there was no room there any longer, but down below by the ocean. The rock had made the graves too shallow, so they had had to bring in extra earth and pile high mounds on top of the graves.

Mammy looked at the graves and then started crying. 'But where is he? Where is he? There are no names here. Look at all the work he did. He was such a good man. He was a man no one ought to forget. Why are there no names here? Have all these people been forgotten?'

It was October. The rain-soaked ground outside their tent had started to freeze up hard every night and then thaw out during the day, churning the mud and grass. They still slept on the bare earth, for fear of damaging the wool blankets they had brought with them from Ireland, their only treasure. Mammy refused to leave and patients were dying of cold. Eamonn could do nothing. His mother refused to believe that the captain was dead. She said he would want her to carry on, helping the sick just as he had done, until he came back.

Dr Douglas visited their tent one night, to talk to her himself and tell her that he had closed the captain's eyes, that they had had to remove the body quickly because of the risk of infection—as they did whenever anyone died. But Eamonn's mother stared at the doctor, with eyes that looked right through him.

'Is your mother well, laddie?'

'She just has these strange ideas, since the captain died. And she keeps staring into the distance, like that. We have to go away from here, doctor. She'll be all right once we get away.'

The doctor put his hand on Mammy's forehead and she started to shiver. 'Are you very cold?' he asked.

'No. Not cold. Too hot. My head aches.'

The doctor lifted her up in his arms.

'No! Leave her here! We can look after her.' Eamonn backed away, blocking the entrance to the tent. 'Don't take her into the hospital. We can look after her so she doesn't die. Everyone dies in there. Everyone dies. Don't take her there!'

Dr Douglas pushed past him and started to stride up the hill, with Eamonn running to keep up with him. 'We can look after her better in a proper room. And you're wrong. People don't always die. Your mother has the strength to survive.'

'Well, I can come and look after her.' Eamonn was out of breath from trying to keep back the tears. 'She won't want to be left on her own.'

Dr Douglas reached the entrance to the hospital and one of the orderlies opened the doors and pushed a wheeled bed towards him.

'Listen, laddie. You're the only one, now, to look after those brothers of yours. Make sure you keep them alive and well. That's your job now.'

But it was Dermot who looked after his older brother that night. Eamonn threw himself onto the cold floor of the tent and sobbed.

They should have left the island then, while they still had time, before the real disaster happened. Dr Douglas told them they should leave. He said that if their mother recovered he would seek them out, wherever they were, and let them know how she was and where she had gone to. He said they should leave the island, before things got worse.

Eamonn didn't know what he was talking about. Yes, it was cold and getting colder every day, but they had seen cold before, and they still hadn't started to use their blankets. They still had money to buy food, and Eamonn had been earning them a little money every day he worked at the hospital. Now the doctor wouldn't let him work there any longer.

'You can't stop me seeing my mother, sir.' Eamonn didn't want to shout at the doctor. He had worked hard for all of them. Where were all the other doctors? Why was there no one to help him? Eamonn could understand why his mother had wanted to stay and help in the hospital. Now that she was a patient too, sick and helpless, there was nowhere else he wanted to be. He couldn't think of the danger, of the numbers of priests and nurses and all the other helpers the sickness had brought down that year. All he could think of was the promises he had made to look after his mother and his two brothers. He couldn't just walk off and leave her. So he stood at the hospital door, shouting at the doctor.

'You can't stop me seeing my mother, sir.'

Dr Douglas opened the door wide. Eamonn could have

rushed past him any time. 'No, I can't stop you seeing your mother, laddie. And I won't stop you seeing her. But I'm asking you now to think of those two, wee boys you've left behind. Who's going to look after them if you get the fever too?'

'Dermot's old enough to look after Shaun. He doesn't need me.'

'Aye, nine years old is old enough, I suppose. But do you want to leave them all alone, with no one?'

He waved his hand to let Eamonn go past him, along the corridor and into the ward.

All the time Eamonn sat beside his mother she didn't recognize him, just lay on her side staring ahead of her at the wall beyond him, or fell asleep and talked in her sleep about places he barely remembered and people he had never known. Once she woke up and called him by his father's name, but then she closed her eyes again.

The ward was quiet. It was growing dark and all the patients were quiet. Eamonn wanted to believe they were all sleeping peacefully. If they were so ill, ill enough to die within a matter of days, shouldn't they be shouting out in pain? Shouldn't they be making some sort of a fuss?

He heard bare feet running and slipping on the waxed floors. Who could be walking around with no shoes on, now that the ground was frozen all the time? A pair of brown boots landed on the floor beside him and Eamonn stared at the boots and then at their owner, then back at his mother.

'Dermot, you've left Shaun alone!'

'Ah, he's all right. He's promised to stay in the tent. I wanted to see what was up with our mammy.' Then he whispered, 'Is she going to get better? She's asleep now, isn't she, Eamonn? She's asleep and not dead, isn't she, Eamonn?'

Eamonn stood up and picked up the brown boots.

'She's asleep. They'll look after her. Now she's in here

with the doctor to look after her, she'll get better. Don't you worry. But we've got to look after Shaun.'

Their mother didn't even notice them walking away, though Dermot's bare feet made a slip-slop sound along the green, shiny waxed floor. Outside, the cold air landed, like a big cat stalking them, clinging to their shoulders. Eamonn heard himself taking charge, calmly telling Dermot to stop and put on his boots, even though another, frantic voice inside his head was telling him everything was lost. What was the point of putting on boots to keep out the cold? There was no point to anything they did. Whatever they did, people were still going to die, were dying all around them. And nothing Eamonn could do was going to stop that, not telling his brother to lace his boots up, not rushing back to the tent to make sure Shaun was safe from being carried off by the fever or the cold, not all the fighting he would have to do to stop the hunger coming back again.

They had run and kept on running, thousands of miles from the place where the hunger had first killed his grandma, his sister, and then his father. They had driven on, through the storms at sea and the lack of food and water and Eamonn had kept them all going, looking after them, making sure they did not give up. But nothing he could do was good enough to stop the people dying.

They walked quickly, along the long side of the hospital buildings. Two new blocks had been built that summer and still there wasn't enough room for all the people. They walked around the chapel, with its few, small gravestones and long, low wall. Most of the graves, he knew, were unmarked, rows of them stretching out to the coast. They walked past the fever sheds and then down the hill to where the tents still struggled to cling to the rocky side of the hill. It was dark now and freezing. No sounds came from any of the tents. People at that time of the night had already huddled together to sleep, to try and keep warm.

'You shouldn't have left Shaun alone,' Eamonn shouted, as they picked their way over tent ropes, the ice and snow crunching under their feet. 'He's too little to be left on his own.'

'But I wanted to know about Mammy,' Dermot's voice was stupid, like a baby's. 'And I was frightened, Eamonn. I don't want her to die.'

Inside the dark tent, Shaun was sitting on Mammy's bundle, full of their best clothes all rolled up for Sunday. He had all of their four blankets wrapped around him, but he pulled off the top two as soon as they sat down on the floor beside him.

'I was only borrowing them,' he said. 'I'm not cold, honest, Eamonn.'

Eamonn picked him up and sat him on his knee. 'Are you all right, Shaun? Are you all right?'

Shaun took his thumb out of his mouth. 'I stayed right here. That's what Dermot said, "Stay right there, Shaun." And I did, didn't I, Dermot?'

'But we can't stay here.' Eamonn rocked his brother on his knee as if he were a much smaller child being rocked to sleep. He put his free arm out to stroke Dermot's shoulder. 'We can't stay here, Dermot, in all this snow and ice.'

Dermot brightened up, now that Eamonn was no longer angry with him. 'I don't mind where we go, Eamonn. We can go wherever you want. As soon as Mammy's better, we can go away and find some place where people don't get ill, can't we, Eamonn? America's full of places where you can get jobs and people don't get ill. And you can get three meals a day.'

Eamonn laughed. 'You're as bad as Daddy used to be, with your fairy tales. What put that one into your head? Three meals a day!'

'Mrs Grogan. On the ship. She said people in America eat three meals a day, regular. And she told us stories about all the food. Didn't she, Shaun?'

Shaun nodded his head, but he was almost fast asleep. That day he had eaten one meal, the food doled out near the fever sheds once a day. But it was enough for a boy who had lived for days in Ireland on blackberries and dandelion leaves.

A bowl of porridge was just enough.

SIX

'The fever is just something you has to live
through.' One of the troop of old women who
gathered every day at the entrance to the hospital,
to collect the washing or wait for news of relatives or
friends, wasn't afraid of the fever any more. 'You just have
to make sure you live through it. And if you manages to
live through it, then you don't die.'

Mrs Lynch did washing for the fever patients. And she
wasn't afraid to do their washing, not like some people
who wouldn't go anywhere near the hospital for fear that
the smell of sickness would kill them. Mrs Lynch wasn't
even afraid to walk into a ward and take the sheets off the
bed where a person had just died and carry them herself
to the wash-house. Mrs Lynch knew the wards inside out
from walking around them to collect washing, from
stopping and chatting to the priests and relatives who
came in and sometimes didn't come out again. And Mrs
Lynch wasn't afraid. She had lived through the fever
herself, given up for lost by her relatives in May, but back
among the living, fit as a fiddle she called it, in June.

That was when she decided she had found the job she
wanted to do in America. Nobody else would do the
washing. Dr Douglas needed the washing done for all of
his patients every day, and as long as she got her money
she was the one to do it. A charmed life she led. Anyone
would say you led a charmed life if you managed to live
through the fever and didn't die.

Mrs Lynch pronounced judgement on all the patients.
While the doctor said it was impossible to tell who might
live and who would definitely not survive, Mrs Lynch
knew better. And her verdict on Eamonn's mother was
that she wasn't the dying sort. She had lived too long with

the fever, for a start. It was the beginning of November, the river had frozen over, no new ships were arriving with their cargoes of fever for the Isle and still, among the last survivors in the hospital ward, Eamonn's mother hovered between a deep sleep and a sort of wakefulness where she didn't really notice them.

They slept inside the hospital now, Eamonn and his brothers and the fifty or more orphan children who had been left stranded at the hospital. It was warmer there and one or two patients were recovering, and Mrs Lynch told Eamonn his mother would soon be among them.

'It's the way she sleeps.' Mrs Lynch stood with folded arms. 'And the way she breathes. Nice deep breaths. Listen.' And she stood, holding her own breath to make sure that Eamonn heard his mother's deep, sighing breathing in the silent ward.

'She's lived with the fever too long.' Mrs Lynch shook her head. 'She's not going to die with it now.' And Eamonn felt reassured by the warmth of the room where they slept. All day long, in the freezing cold, he worked hard, helping the doctor's men clear up the mud and filth around the tents and sort out the tents to see which could be used the next time around if more cases of fever arrived in spring. There were graves to be shored up too, rows and rows of graves within sight of the ocean, where earth still had to be piled up and the ground around made tidy.

Every day his mother held on was one day more she had lived with the fever. Mrs Lynch said her breathing was getting better all the time.

Then Dr Douglas took him aside.

'We're closing the hospital soon, for winter, laddie. There'll be no more ships now until spring.'

'Will our mother be able to go somewhere else?'

'We won't be making anyone move. We'll be staying here as long as we're needed.' The doctor walked with a stick now, and he sat down heavily on the straw mattress of an empty bed, balancing his stick carefully against the metal rungs. 'I want you to think about something for me.'

Eamonn scuffed with his boots on the shiny green floor. They were the grand, shiny boots the doctor had given him from some other boy who wouldn't be needing them any more.

'There are some good people coming here tomorrow, all the way from a church in Quebec.'

Eamonn bent down and undid one of his shoelaces, slowly taking the laces right out of all the holes and then just as slowly lacing them back in again.

'They've heard of our orphans, here on the island. The bishop himself preached them a sermon, as far as I know. Are you listening to me, laddie?'

Eamonn nodded, keeping his head still bent over, his lace only up to the third hole.

'They're all going to take children with them, Eamonn. Treat them like their own sons and daughters. These Canadian people are going to take you all and bring you up as if you were their own.'

Eamonn stopped and looked up. 'Not us. We're not orphans.' Then he carried on again, concentrating on his shoelaces.

'They are all good people, Eamonn. They'd have to be good people, to take on poor Irish orphans and bring them up as if they were their own flesh and blood.'

Eamonn finished doing up one of his boots and sat down on the floor, his hands wrapped round his knees. The warm socks he had on came from the doctor too. He had never seen such long, thick socks in Ireland where it was never as cold as November in Canada.

'We can stay here, can't we? Until spring. Then our mother will be better and we can set off for America. I can do the work for you, like I have been doing.'

'I have to go to my family, Eamonn. I haven't seen my wife or my family since the spring of this year.'

'Why can't they come here?'

The doctor shook his head.

'But we can stay here. And when our mother gets well, she can clean for you too. We can all work to help you here.'

The doctor stroked the back of Eamonn's hand. 'It's better for you and your brothers if you go now, while there's a chance to get settled with a family to look after you and care for you.'

'We can't leave our mother.'

'I will be here to look after her as long as she needs looking after. I can let you know how she is, if you want me to.'

'You mean she can come and get us as soon as she's well?'

Dr Douglas nodded. 'It will be a long time, if she gets well, before she can travel. But—'

'But she'll miss us here. She'll want to know where we are.'

'It's best for you to go, Eamonn. While you have the chance. They are good people, the ones who are coming here tomorrow. All good people from the church. Someone has to take care of you and your brothers, Eamonn.'

'I can take care of myself.'

A priest was the first to arrive, the next day. It was a Tuesday and the whole of Grosse Isle was quiet, apart from the sound of the spades and pickaxes, hacking away at the frozen earth, as the men worked hard to dig the last few graves deep enough into the ground.

Father Roach made the children stand in rows, from the tallest down to the smallest. Eamonn was away from both his brothers but he could see them in front of him, Dermot at the far end of the second row, Shaun sitting down now in front, holding hands with Maire O'Sullivan whose mother had died of the fever the day before. Maire was four and had cried for two days when her mother was first taken into the hospital. But it had all happened very quickly with her. Now the little girl didn't seem to know who she belonged to. She had copper-red curls tumbling all over the shoulders of the long black dress they had found for her. She was proud of her shiny, black lace-up boots and showed them to anyone who stopped near her.

When the people started to arrive, some couples in black buggies with sleek black horses, some whole families on sledges pulled by horses, the children broke out of their rows and rushed to the windows, pointing excitedly as each new wagon drew up and the drivers jumped out and tied up their horses alongside the hospital building. It was as if there was going to be a grand party there. The hospital had never had so many visitors.

Father Roach and Dr Douglas, in a dark suit instead of the white coat they usually saw him wearing, rushed out to greet their guests. Mrs Lynch had been given the job of providing them all with hot drinks and warm cake and she ran round serving them in the great entrance hall, handing out drinks of hot coffee and cakes and stories of how the fever ran through the camp and which little orphans had had a worse time of it. As she took round the platters of cake for the second time she told the story of her own fight with the fever and how you just had to live through the fever and then it wouldn't kill you. And a man in a grey morning coat, who had left a fur wrap out in the entrance hall, asked Father Roach was it all right to ask a question.

The visitors sat down, on hard chairs in the centre, on the sofas and armchairs around the side of what would have been the doctors' reading room if ever there had been enough doctors on Grosse Isle to make the hospital a place where doctors had had time to sit and study. Most of the visitors were neighbours from the same small town. They carried on chatting, about the cold, the cost of keeping the cows indoors and the time it took for washing to dry. Some of the families came from remote farms and only met up with the others once a week when they made the long journey to church. All of them had come to take home an orphan child.

The man in the grey morning coat stood up in front of the fire under the window at the far end of the room. He raised the tails of his coat, warming his legs against the fire. He was at home in the large, comfortable room, as if it was his own living room and he was in charge. And he had been listening carefully to Mrs Lynch's stories.

'Tell me, Father,' he said, 'or maybe the doctor can tell us. All the children we are going to see have lost their parents to the fever?'

'That is correct.'

'And some people—the lady we see here, the good lady who has been kind enough to serve us with refreshments—some people have managed to survive the fever with no apparent ill-effects?'

Father Roach turned to the doctor, who nodded. 'A few, a very few people have survived once they have taken the infection.'

'So these children all come from very weak stock?'

The room went quiet. There were no teaspoons stirring. Mrs Lynch stood still, a plate in her hand, when she had just been about to put it down on her pile.

They all kept cattle and horses. They knew what it meant when the man talked about weak stock. It meant animals from sickly parents, animals that were always going to be sick themselves. Cost a fortune in bills from the veterinary, if you could get one in the middle of winter.

'Can you assure us, doctor, that none of these children are already infected with the fever or some other illness that could destroy our healthy families? In all Christian charity, we want to help. We are here to help, but . . . '

'They have survived when everyone around them was getting the illness,' Dr Douglas said. 'If you were to ask me, I would say they are pretty healthy stock, myself.' The words they used, the animal words to describe the children he had watched and cared for as much as he could in the middle of all the catastrophe of that summer, froze the air between them. The doctor disliked the man in the grey frock-coat. He was suspicious of these people, all of them enquiring after his children as if they were at some sort of a cattle market. But the children needed homes. And the people who had come were farmers with land and enough food to feed an extra mouth.

Dr Douglas had more things on his mind. There were fifty-three children, and sixty couples had arrived. The hospital had never had to cater for such a large group of healthy, able-bodied people before. Mrs Lynch was carrying cups and saucers backwards and forwards between the kitchen and the doctors' reading room and through that room into the lounge. There was simply not enough space.

'We will be keeping brothers and sisters together, Father?'

Father Roach moved away from the doctor, shaking hands with families from other parishes, people he had only met before at Christmas dances or the last bishop's funeral. Dr Douglas followed him.

'I need to have a word with you, if you please, Father.'

Father Roach moved with the doctor over to the far door, leading to a wide corridor and then to the wards.

'I promised the parents these children would stay together, Father. We cannot allow them to split up brother and sister, can we now?'

Father Roach gave a low whistle and then bit his lip. 'These are very good people, you know, doctor.' He shook his head. 'But that would be asking too much of them, three children—sometimes four or five. We'll have to see what happens.'

Then Father Roach went through to the ward where the children were still waiting, bored now with staring out of the window at the fine carriages and the horses. He clapped his hands and the children waiting jumped back into place, into the five rows he had put them in before according to age and height.

'Right, little ones, come with me and we'll see what cake there is left for you.' The first row of children, Shaun and Maire holding hands, ran along out of the room with Father Roach.

'It's not fair,' Dermot shouted. 'There'll be no cake left by the time we get there.' And he knew what cake he was talking about. Mrs Lynch and the kitchen women had started their baking on Sunday, and Shaun had eaten the first cake he could ever remember.

The next ten children were called for so quickly that Eamonn still thought they were simply letting them come into the great rooms gradually, as they had done on board ship when they were giving out food or water, to make sure everyone got some cake. It was only right to leave the oldest until last. He crept away at the far end of the ward and walked through the remaining three wards. Now they were almost empty. Maire's mother had been the last new case of fever. The others, the ten women in Mammy's ward and the men in the one next along, had been sick for longer.

Mammy turned towards him as he got close to her bed.

'Eamonn! You look as if you've had something to eat at last!' She smiled. 'Has someone been fattening you up to take you to market?'

He sat down beside her and held her hand. He had no idea how long he sat there, smiling at his mother, willing her to get better, while she smiled back at him, looking straight at him, not vaguely towards the wall behind him, but straight into his eyes. Now everything would be all right. Now no one could make them go away and leave her.

'How do you feel, Mammy? Are you getting better now? You're getting better, aren't you?'

She smiled at him and squeezed his hand.

He suddenly realized that they might be looking for him. 'Wait. I'll go and get the doctor. So he can see how much better you are.'

Eamonn turned and ran, ran along the path between the row of narrow beds and through into the next quiet ward, then along the corridor that backed onto the ward where he had left Dermot with all the other children.

They were gone. The greedy rascals must have eaten all the cake. Eamonn opened the door into the next long corridor, the one that led to the doctors' private rooms. It was quiet there too, but he glanced out of the window which overlooked the side of the main hospital wing. The bells on the chapel clock struck four. The horses and carriages were all gone. The sledges had disappeared—all except one carriage and a sledge with two ice-grey horses.

Eamonn didn't understand. Where were all the children? Where were his brothers? He crept past the kitchen, where Mrs Lynch and two of the women who sometimes came to help her were up to their elbows in soap suds, clattering the plates and cutlery in the deep stone sinks and laughing about the clothes that some of the farmers had been wearing.

Then he pushed open the door of the doctors' reading room, a room he had never been allowed to enter. Three men stood with their backs to him, two of them propping themselves up against the mantelpiece, one staring into the fire. Dr Douglas turned round.

'Just the laddie we've been looking for.'

'Our mother is going to get well, sir.'

The doctor shook his head. 'I've been to see her today, laddie.'

'She was lying there smiling and looking at me.' Then Eamonn ran to the window. 'Where are the others?

Where are Shaun and Dermot? She'll want to see them, now she can see properly. She spoke to me. She knows who I am.'

Father Roach took Eamonn by the shoulders, turned him away from the window and steered him back towards the fire. 'This is Mr Buchanan, Eamonn. He and his wife were good enough to say they will take an older boy.' Then he laughed. 'Even though everyone knows that boys your age never stop eating.'

Eamonn looked at the man in the grey morning coat, lifting his coat-tails up again now and warming himself at the fire as he stared at Eamonn. Then he turned to Dr Douglas. 'Where is Shaun? Where are my brothers?'

'They've gone with good people, Eamonn. They'll have a good life. You musn't worry yourself. They're with good, Catholic families.'

It was as if Eamonn had fainted and then been brought back to consciousness. He didn't fall over. But for some time he didn't know the world. He froze. He saw nothing. He heard nothing. He had no idea how long he stayed like that. Then he came to.

He looked at the three men, all towering above him. Two of them smiling, convinced they were doing what was best for him. They had taken his brothers away from him. He had promised his father he would look after the family and now they had taken his brothers away. Still no words came. He wanted to turn and run. He wanted to spit and scratch and kick out at the smiling men. But he froze and stared instead at Dr Douglas.

The doctor took the other two men aside and then came back to Eamonn, guiding him over to the window and sitting down beside him on one of the soft, flower-covered sofas which had never been used until that day.

'I can find out for you, Eamonn, where your brothers have gone. You don't have to lose touch with them. And your mother will be all right here with me. We won't be closing up the hospital until all our charges are discharged.'

'And when she's better, you'll tell me, so I can come and get her?'

'I'll always give you news of her, as soon as you write to me.'

Splinters of ice clung to Eamonn's hair, where the fast flying flakes from a snowstorm had first soaked him through and then floated away, left behind them like the miles and miles of road after the ferry had taken them off Grosse Isle. Eamonn put his hand up and pulled at the ice, but more seemed to form as soon as he pulled one piece away. Mr Buchanan stared ahead at the dark road, not bothering to talk. Eamonn cried when he thought of his mother, waking up in the dark hospital ward and calling out for him. But the tears turned to ice.

He put his hands under the blanket Mr Buchanan had drawn up over their knees, but nothing could make him warmer. The grey horses shone in the icy moonlight. On and on they drove, with hardly a light or a house anywhere near. Soon Eamonn was dead to the cold.

They drew up outside a long, low house made of thick logs, with a roof that hung down to the ground, all thatched with snow and with lacy, ice-patterned gables. Nobody came out to meet them and Eamonn could see no lights. He watched as Mr Buchanan unhooked the horses, hung up their saddles and bridles and rubbed them down. Then he settled them, by the light of a very small lamp, with food and water in the barn. The first warm sound in that place was the sound of the horses chomping at their food, tossing straw over their backs and settling down for the night.

As long as Mr Buchanan said nothing, Eamonn didn't know what to say to him. His thoughts were miles away, with his mother in hospital on the island and with his brothers, wherever they were. He didn't even know whether they were together or not. He wanted most of all to know that they were together, that at least Dermot was around to look after Shaun.

They walked across the frozen yard to the back door of the house. Mr Buchanan took a huge key off a hook on the wall and opened the door which whined like a dog left alone too long. Inside, the house was quiet and dark and cold.

'Can you feel your way around?' Mr Buchanan was taking his shoes off and Eamonn did the same, taking his time with the long black laces on his boots, his fingers too wooden to work. His feet stung from the cold.

'There's a door here, on the left. That's where you can sleep, till Mrs finds you a bed from somewhere else. Maybe there's one somewhere around no one wants.' His strange accent was more Scottish than American when he whispered.

Inside the cupboard door was a ladder which led up to a top shelf, just long enough for Eamonn to stretch out flat. Someone had laid some sweet-smelling straw all over the shelf and there was a thick, goose-down quilt to go on top.

'Mrs'll wake you up in the morning early.'

Then Mr Buchanan shut the door and Eamonn heard his stockinged feet shuffle away along the corridor to where he opened another door and was gone. The cupboard was pitch dark. The whole house was pitch dark and the shelf bed was quiet and warm and comfortable. As Eamonn fell asleep, he ran back along the corridors between the ward where he had stayed with his mother and forgotten the time and the doctors' library, where fifty children had suddenly disappeared and gone away. He ran back to look for the time he had lost, the time it had taken for them to steal his brothers away.

He dreamt that his brothers, too, were shut up in dark cupboards, hammering on the doors and calling out his name, pleading with him to let them out and take them home. In the middle of one of his dreams, a hand grabbed hold of his shoulder and shook him and turned him roughly around from his front onto his back. Eamonn put up his hands to protect his face and then lay there, staring, with his fists curled over his mouth.

A girl stood on the top rung of the ladder to his cupboard-bed, her head inside the cupboard so that her face was half in darkness. But Eamonn could see that she was staring at him. She touched her fingers to his right eye and then to his left eye, stroking them closed and then watching as he slowly opened them again. Eamonn wanted to scream but he knew of no one in the house who would hear him scream. For the first minute he had forgotten how he came there.

He was warm under the goose-down quilt, but he shivered. The girl touched his cheek and then a man's voice called out, 'Katharina, what are you doing now? Where are you?'

The girl took no notice of the shouting, didn't even seem to hear it. Then it came again, from down at the far end of the long house. 'Katharina, are you with the boy?'

Eamonn jerked his head to the right where the voice was coming from and then the girl turned too. She put her fingers to her lips to silence Eamonn, ducked her head down, and disappeared down the ladder. Eamonn remembered the man's voice from the night before. It was Mr Buchanan.

'I might have known I'd find you there.'

But the girl said nothing.

There was clean, warm water to wash in. Katharina brought water in a large, pink-flowered bowl to the room in between the kitchen and Eamonn's shelf-bed. Then she gave him a towel and some soap and closed the door as she left the room. The house was quiet and the water slipped warm over Eamonn's hands and face. The house was so quiet.

Eamonn squeezed out the linen cloth and smoothed it over the back of his hand, as if he were smoothing a cloth over his mother's brow, one of the cold linen cloths they had used to take down the fever. Who would be there to look after her now? Perhaps that was a sign that the doctor was sure of her getting well, letting the three boys go, with no one else to look after her when everyone had said Eamonn made such a grand job of it. There was a knock on the door and Mr Buchanan walked in, not the grand man in his grey morning coat now, but wearing a collarless shirt and a thick tweed jacket.

'Water? You've had a wash? Good. Mrs Buchanan will give you some breakfast.'

Then he went out, closing the heavy back door of the house and crossing the yard to the stables. Eamonn opened the door of the small room next to the kitchen and stepped out into the stone-flagged corridor. The kitchen door was closed. Eamonn knocked on the door but there was no answer. He was sure someone must be in the kitchen because of what Mr Buchanan said. He knocked again, and then called out, 'Hello!' His voice echoed around the corridor but there was no answer.

Eamonn opened the kitchen door. The girl, Katharina, sat with her back to him, head in her hands, elbows on the table. She took no notice of him entering the room, so he said again, 'Hello. Good morning to you.' Still she didn't turn round. Through the long, low window, Eamonn saw Mr Buchanan emerge into the yard. From the outside he opened the tall double doors to the barn where the sledge was kept. Then he came out of the stable part of the barn pulling the two grey horses and hitched them up to the sledge.

Katharina jumped up and ran to the window, smiling and pointing at the beautiful horses and their owner, moving her head from side to side. But no sound came out of her talking, smiling mouth. She was a beautiful girl, with two long blonde plaits coiled to a crown on the top of her head and she had jewel-blue eyes. Eamonn never heard her speak.

When she turned round from the window, she saw Eamonn and ran over to him and took his hand, leading him to the table. Then she stood and served him, with pancakes and syrup and coffee and oat porridge. And Eamonn, who hadn't eaten properly since they had left their last safe base in Ireland, had in the end to smile and put his hand over his cup and his plate and have a mock fight with her until she recognized that he had had enough to eat and could not, could not eat any more.

Then Katharina held out her hand and led Eamonn to a darkened room at the front of the house. The curtains were closed, but the light of a roaring fire meant they could see the small woman lying on the day-bed before she turned and saw them.

'You've eaten, young man?'

Eamonn thanked her for his food and the warm bed.

'I cannot take company for too long.' Mrs Buchanan patted one of her pillows and Katharina jumped forward and rearranged it. 'You're here to help Katharina,' she said then, 'until you're big enough and strong enough to help my husband with the outside work.'

Eamonn was glad to escape from the dark, overheated room. And Katharina only began to smile again after she had shut the door behind her. After that, the same thing happened every day. They went to see Mrs Buchanan for a short time in the morning and again in the evening before they went to bed. And every time they saw her, Eamonn felt as if everything he said, every movement either of them made, caused her pain. He couldn't wait to get away from the sick woman.

Katharina showed him how to help her hang the washing up, in a long, roofed-in balcony at the edge of the house. She showed him piled up wood that had to be carried in and stacked next to the fire. Eamonn asked her questions about herself and about the house, about her mother and father and about whether they had any neighbours. When he was facing her and she could see that he was talking she smiled at him and nodded but that was the only response he ever got.

Mr Buchanan came home long after dark every night, said grace, ate his dinner with the two of them, read from the gospels, went to see his wife and soon afterwards took up the lantern and told them it was time for bed. He wasn't a man you could question, unless you got him at the right time, maybe. And there never was a right time for the questions Eamonn wanted to ask him. Why does Katharina never speak or listen? Has she always been like that? She isn't stupid, is she? What is the job that you do, that keeps you away all day and long into the evening? Where have they taken my brothers? Are they near here? Maybe they're in a valley just over the hill? And what has happened to my mother? When will this winter end and when can I go and look for my family?

There was never a right time for the questions. Eamonn was given good food and, soon enough, a comfortable, narrow bed in his own small room. He had work to do too, but not too much work, helping Katharina in the house, making sure her mother was well and looking after the animals all day while Mr Buchanan was away. The world outside was quiet, so quiet that Eamonn learned to recognize the calls of different birds and foxes. Alone all day with Katharina, sometimes working alongside her but just as often working on his own out at the edge of the forest, he thought he too had forgotten how to speak.

He talked to himself, or talked to Shaun and Dermot and their mother far away. He spoke out loud, when he was far away from the house, trying out his voice, hearing himself telling his mother he was well and had enough to eat. He knew that people would say he was going mad, the way he talked to himself, but there was no one else to talk to.

On Sundays, when they went to church, the world was suddenly loud, with singing and families talking for what seemed like hours. And then there was quiet again, on the long road back to their house, with only the clip clop of the horses' hooves and the swoosh of the sledge over the ice. And sometimes Mr Buchanan would break the silence, pointing to animals he saw in the woods by the track. 'Fox over there. White. Just about see it.' Katharina always stared straight ahead if he looked to the right, or she looked to the side if he pointed to something out in front of them. Mrs Buchanan never left the house.

There never was a right time to ask Eamonn's questions. And there were always more questions to ask. One Sunday in church he heard the priest praise the families who had rescued Irish orphans. But where were all the others? Fifty Irish children had left the hospital the day he did, but not one of them was at the church he went to. Where had they gone to, and where were Dermot and Shaun? The priest said, 'The Irish are among the most debased of immigrants, the most debased of our poor. But, brothers and sisters, you didn't shrink from taking them into your homes. Bringing them up as your own flesh and blood.'

What did he mean when he called them debased? They hadn't done anything wrong.

One night Mr Buchanan gave him the answer to some of the questions he hadn't been able to ask. One Monday night it was, after Eamonn had helped him to feed and wipe down the horses and clear the snow off the sledge. He drank far more than his usual small glass of whisky and talked far more than Eamonn had ever heard him. Katharina got up to go to bed, but Mr Buchanan motioned to Eamonn to sit down again and talk to him.

'Nobody ever talks to me round here.' He was cold and angry. 'Why does nobody say anything?' Then he was quiet for a long time, staring at the fire he had stoked up instead of damping it down for the night. 'I want you to stay and talk to me, Eamonn, because it's ten years ago it happened. You know all about it?'

Eamonn shook his head.

'I thought they might have told you. At the church. I had a son then. Three years old. Walking and talking. And my wife was happy then, ten years ago.'

He raised his right foot and pointed towards the alcove at the far side of the table. 'My son was sleeping. Sleeping right there in his little bed near the fire, to keep him warm.'

He took a sip of his whisky and banged the glass down on the table. Then he looked over his shoulder towards the door as if he was expecting his wife to walk in. 'Katharina was with me in the barn, seeing to the animals. You never heard anyone talk as much as she did then. She was five. So there we were talking and laughing. And we heard them coming. Raiders.'

'Indians?'

'No. Not Indians. They're peaceful settlers round here, Indians. No. It was white men raiding. I heard twenty horses. The men were shouting and laughing and drunk. So I grabbed Katharina's hand and ran with her to the stone passage under the house. All the houses round here have one.'

He stopped and stared into the fire again. 'She was screaming about the baby and her mother and I had to stop her. They had guns and they were shooting around, wild with them. I reckoned they were after money or the animals and they might not notice the baby.' He swigged from his whisky glass again and wiped his hand across his mouth. 'I had to put my hand over Katy's mouth to stop her, hold her mouth so tight that she bit me.' He held his hand up to the light of the lamp and showed Eamonn the curved, half-moon scar.

'We were lucky they didn't burn us out. But they ripped the house to pieces. We waited till it was quiet, and it was deadly quiet when we got out there. They took the animals and they took the baby. And they knocked my wife out cold.' Again he turned and looked towards the door. 'I haven't heard a sound out of Katharina ever since.'

Then he raised his glass to Eamonn. 'My son would be the same age as you, if he were still around.'

Eamonn went to his bed soon after that, leaving Mr Buchanan sitting alone by the kitchen fire. But he didn't fall asleep. He lay there listening to the quiet outside, a quiet that held the screeching of foxes, owls, and terrified mice calling, and further and further away, the noise of raiders' horses and Katharina's screams the night they killed her brother. He knew he couldn't stay there.

He had food enough and a warm quilt to cover him at night. After the two years when food had been so hard to get, he knew people would say he was stupid to even think of leaving when he got three good meals a day with the Buchanans. But he needed money and he wanted to make his own way.

He needed money more than he needed three good meals a day and a warm bed. He wanted to earn the sort of money people had told him you could get in America, so he could find his brothers and they could all together go back to Grosse Isle and get their mother. He wanted to send his brothers to school and make a home for them all. And in the end, not straight away, but sometime when they had settled everything, he wanted to send the money back to Kate in Ireland, all the money she had given them to make their journey. He wanted to show her how well they'd managed to do and make her proud of him. All of that had to be possible, if it were true what people said about what you could earn, how a person could do well for themselves in America if they weren't afraid of hard work.

He knew he couldn't stay there. He wasn't earning money. After weeks of working outside on his own and in the house with Katharina, he thought he was going mad and forgetting how to talk. And after the night when Mr Buchanan drank and talked and drank until he'd said more than he ever wanted to say, he and his wife hardly talked to Eamonn any more. Eamonn knew he couldn't stay there. That wasn't what he'd journeyed all the way to America for—to waste away in a forgotten corner of a forest, with enough to eat and a warm bed but with people half-crazed by the loneliness of the place.

He wanted work and money, and a way to get his family back together.

SEVEN

'What are you up to, young man?'
Father Moylan spent his Sunday mornings after mass chatting to the families who came to talk about baptisms and weddings. Eamonn sat, undisturbed, beside Father Moylan's bookshelves, while Mr Buchanan stood and gossiped with other parish men and Katharina helped the housekeeper to make warm drinks before people set off back to their farms.

'I'm sorry, Father. I thought you didn't mind me looking at your books.'

After six months in North America, Eamonn still had no idea where he was. He knew their ship had landed them in Canada, not in America—because of the number of sick people they knew they had on board. But he had the idea in his head that Canada was just a matter of an hour's walk to Boston, if only he knew which way to walk.

'Not at all. Not at all, young man. Look at all the books you want. Have you no books at home? You can take some home if you want and bring them back next Sunday. Whatever you want to read.'

Eamonn didn't want to take a book away with him. He wanted to get away that week, as soon as the rivers looked like thawing. Taking a book home would mean staying on longer, reading books and having to return them and getting used to three good meals a day. He sat and stared at the Atlas he had taken down from the shelves. He knew that maps were supposed to tell you where to go, but he didn't know how you could work things out from a flat, green and brown picture with blue all around it. The blue was the sea, he could tell that, but there was sea on either side of the land and he didn't know which part of the sea it was that they had sailed.

Then the map started to make sense. He suddenly found Grosse Isle on the map, and a line on the sea which said, 'To Liverpool', and then an arrow pointing downwards which said 'To Boston'. But how would he know which way was down if he walked out of the Buchanan's long, wooden house? Did he walk into the forest and just keep walking? Or should he keep to the track that would lead him to the church.

Father Moylan walked up behind him. 'Ah, it's geography now, you're interested in, is it? And where in the world are you planning to go?'

Eamonn blushed and looked quickly over to where Mr Buchanan was standing with his back to the fire, warming himself. 'I just thought I could tell where we are. And where Boston is. But they never taught us maps, the priests that taught me how to read and write.'

Father Moylan laughed and spoke to the group of men near the fire. 'Did you hear that? Our young man from Ireland says they never taught him maps.' Then he smiled at Eamonn. 'They never thought you'd be needing maps, I suppose, when all you were ever going to do was grow potatoes.'

Then he leaned over the large book that Eamonn had spread out on the table and showed him, pointing out of the window as he did so. 'Over there's east, so that way is west. Did they teach you that in Ireland, a big tall boy like you?' Eamonn shook his head.

'We are here, right now. And—who do you live with, remind me? The Buchanans? They're up the track there, five miles from here, north as far as I can tell.'

Eamonn almost whispered, 'And Boston?'

'What on earth do you want to know about Boston for? Isn't Quebec far enough away for you?'

'I've an aunt who lives in Boston.'

Eamonn pointed to the arrow on the map and then out of the window. 'I suppose Boston is down that way? I might visit her when I'm older.'

Father Moylan burst out laughing. 'You could go to Boston that way. That's the quickest way, if you could fly with the crows. But you wouldn't like the country you'd have to get through. No. The best way to get to Boston, when you're older and if ever Buchanans can spare you for a week or two, is to get yourself to St John and then on the Eastern Railroad. That's the only way to go. It's way too far to walk.' And he laughed out loud again.

The only way to leave Buchanan's farm was to slip out during the day, when Mr Buchanan was out on the business that kept him away until nightfall. As soon as he was in the house, he locked the doors. And anyway, night was not the time to travel round the forest.

On Monday, Eamonn walked to the edge of the trail that led to their church. The woods were quiet and beautiful and Katharina waved, smiling at him. He couldn't leave her when there was wood to be chopped and the straw to be moved from the top part of the barn to the far end. She cooked pork that night and Eamonn helped her clean the potatoes. The kitchen was warm and smelt of roast and baking. He must be a fool to leave all that behind.

But they were not his people. And he wasn't doing what he had promised to do. He had no idea where his brothers were. He had left his mother behind, in the hospital. He had to look after his family, his own people.

On Tuesday, he turned back to look at the house and stood and looked at it for a long time. People knew where he was. If anyone came looking for him, if Dermot asked the people he was with to help him find his brother, if Dr Douglas wanted to let him know that his mother was well, Father Moylan could tell them he was with Buchanans. Everyone knew Buchanans had taken an Irish boy, the same age as their lost son would have been. If Eamonn's family started to look for him, they would soon know where he was. No one would ever be able to find him if he went away.

Katharina walked out to the fork in the path, bringing him cake she had baked and he walked back into the house with her. Perhaps he should stay there, after all, just in case his brothers came looking for him.

But on Wednesday he set off early, while Katharina was out at the far side of the barn, feeding the hens. There was no time to waste. His brothers were too young to come for him, his mother perhaps still too ill. There was no time to waste. It was up to him to earn money and bring the family together again. And he could only do that if he got to Boston.

He had no idea how far it was. He had no idea how he was going to get there. He had good, stout boots on, a warm coat and two apples in his pocket. And he set off walking, quickly.

Eamonn had had enough of walking and weary searching for food. And he was on his own now. There was no one to joke with him and remind him why he was making the journey. He knew he was going in the right direction because for much of the way carters and men clearing loads of logs had stopped and told him to hop up alongside them so that he had covered the miles quickly.

But he hadn't realized how long the journey was going to be. And every mile the road stretched out behind him was taking him further away from his brothers and his mother. When the men who took him part of the way asked him where he was going, he always told them, 'To see my aunt in Boston. Mary Kennedy.' But none of the drivers knew Mary Kennedy and none of them had ever been anywhere near Boston.

At the railroad station at St John there were Irish Sunday clothes and Irish accents mingling with the Canadian and French. The Doyles had ten grand boxes and baskets and a maidservant for their small children. They had four small children and one small maidservant who was scared to death of losing one of the ten boxes she had to keep an eye on while Mr and Mrs Doyle went to an office to check that their ticket reservations were in order.

Eamonn stood beside the white fence, next to the entrance to the station. He had been standing there for four hours, ever since he had helped a man with a huge load of logs by watching over the load until the men could move them onto the train. As he watched the logger turn his wagon and just before he set off back the way he had come, Eamonn asked him the same question he had asked everyone who had helped him on his journey.

'How far is it to Boston?'

The first man, who had come upon him on the track away from the Buchanans' house and had taken him to the next town where there was a horse market, shrugged his shoulders and laughed. 'Boston? That's the other end of the world, that is. Why would anyone want to go to Boston?'

The man at the railroad station shook his head and said, 'It's a fair journey, youngster, even if you had a horse and cart, which you haven't. Can't you write that aunt of yours and get her to send you some money so's you can go on the train?'

Eamonn stood at the gate to the station and stared wearily at the comings and goings on the platform without knowing what he was looking at. He had come so far and still the journey would take days, possibly weeks. He had been stupid to leave the safety of the Buchanans' house. His brothers might even be searching for him now, with his mother too.

A little boy, a four year old in velvet knee breeches and with a cap of short black hair that had been polished until it shone, pushed in between Eamonn and the gatepost and walked off down the alleyway beside the station fence, in the direction of a pigsty. The great steam engine had started to hiss and gasp out smoke, but you could still hear the squealing of the piglets through the station fence. Eamonn glanced at the little boy who had squatted down next to the gateway to the pigsty and was pushing pieces of straw through the gaps. He had time to notice that the little boy's fine clothes were already covered in straw-spiked mud. Then he looked back towards the train. All he had to do was to earn some money, find some way of working his passage on the train.

He had been right to move on from the farm. His brothers might never manage to get away from the families who had taken them. They would never see each other again unless he did something about bringing them together. That meant finding work and getting enough money to find them all a place to live. The steam train whistled and Eamonn watched the stokers, stripped to the waist in spite of the raw March cold outside, their faces red hot, with sweat pouring down their backs.

Doors were opening and passengers kissed those waiting on the platform, stored their bags and boxes on top or inside the carriages, and climbed inside. Eamonn caught sight of blue velvet cushions and glass lampshades and then doors were slammed. He thought about jumping onto the step of the train as it pulled away from the station, but there was a ticket collector inside the gate. No one could walk in past him.

The Doyles' maidservant, Rose, looked up in relief as her master and mistress emerged from the station office with the stationmaster in his top hat and coat-tails. 'I've been counting the bags and boxes, all the time you was away, Mrs,' she said, dropping a little curtsy. Mrs Doyle nodded and smiled at her, then put out her two hands to the nearest children.

Rose picked up the smallest one and was just about to scream when Mr Doyle turned round. 'And where's that rascal Jimmy? Where's he hiding now?'

Eamonn watched as the Doyles ran up and down the platform, opening and closing carriage doors, knocking on the doors of waiting rooms, taking out luggage and putting it back in again. It was only when the train engine was letting off great clouds of steam, the stationmaster waved his flag, and the screams of the whole family were drowned in the massive noise of the engine that Eamonn connected their panic with the grubby little boy in his velvet suit, still kneeling on the ground beside the pigsty.

'Jimmy!' he called. But the little boy took no notice. Eamonn ran up to him. 'Jimmy! Your mammy and daddy are calling for you. Come with me.'

And Eamonn grabbed his hand and ran with him to the station entrance. The ticket collector stood back to let them through as the two boys ran towards Jimmy's parents and the whole family got onto the train.

'Come along. You'll miss the train if you go looking for the right carriage. You'd better get into ours till the next halt.' Mr Doyle took Eamonn's hand to shake it and thank him for finding Jimmy just at the moment when the signalman lowered his flag and the stationmaster blew the whistle that set the train in motion. 'Jump in quick, or you'll miss the train, and all because you went looking for our wayward boy.'

Eamonn jumped in and was settled in between Mr and Mrs Doyle who spent the next five minutes alternately scolding Jimmy for getting his clothes in a mess and praising Eamonn for rescuing him just in time.

'What will your cousins say, when we get to Boston and they see you looking like something out of the bog?' Mrs Doyle mopped her eyes. 'We didn't come all this way, half across the world, to lose you.'

Then they turned their attention to Eamonn. 'And where are you travelling to, young man?' Mr Doyle pointed to the carriage wall behind him. 'I suppose your parents know you managed to catch the train after all. Or are you travelling with your master? Never mind, you can get off and join them when we make our first stop. Are they back there?'

'I wasn't supposed to be on the train.' Eamonn stood up, but there was nothing he could do, now he was already inside the moving carriage. 'I have to save our money for when we get to Boston. I wasn't going to take the train.'

The children suddenly stopped talking and tickling each other and stared at him.

'Well, how were you going to get there—wherever you're going?' Mrs Doyle hugged the youngest one on her lap.

'I'm going to Boston, if I can get there. I suppose I was going to walk.'

'And what did your parents say about that?'

'There's only our mammy left, and she's too sick. I have to find work to look after us all.'

'God bless us!' Mrs Doyle kissed the baby until he squirmed and squealed. 'We can't have the boy walking all that way. Mr Doyle will pay for your fare, now won't you, dear?'

'Well, we certainly can't have him walking.'

Eamonn sank back and relaxed in the soft, blue velvet cushions.

EIGHT

'What do you think you're doing here?'

The policeman who woke Eamonn up as he lay, crouched under a tree by the river, towered above him. Eamonn blinked and closed his eyes against the hot sun that came through the branches of the huge old tree.

'I was just sleeping, sir.'

'Well, run along home then. It's nearly eight o'clock. Your mom and dad will be wanting to know where you've been.'

Eamonn slowly got to his feet, rolled up his overcoat and picked up his boots, tied in a knot together so they wouldn't get lost. Then he slung his boots over his shoulder and walked slowly away towards the bridge.

He had been in Boston for two months and it was the first time he had been moved on from the tree where he slept every night.

He was hungry, but he never ate in the evenings. He made himself wait for morning and then feasted on the scraps he found to eat behind the guest houses or outside the university students' refectory. He looked behind him. The tall policeman was still standing under Eamonn's tree, watching him as he walked away. He knew he would have to find somewhere else to sleep, at least for that night.

No one in Boston had ever heard of his aunt, Mary Kennedy. Or if they did know of a Mary Kennedy and Eamonn tramped to the far side of the city and the suburbs to look for her, she would turn out to be the wrong one, a stranger who had never heard of his father and mother and the way they were driven out of their village. The address on the letters his aunt had sent to

Ireland belonged to a row of houses that had been pulled down the year before after some stairs inside collapsed. Even in Boston, Eamonn knew he would have to help himself.

He had looked in shop windows all over Boston, scanned the advertisements on public noticeboards and called on churches and schools and factories offering to do whatever work was needed. Over and over again, when he caught sight of a notice in large black letters, 'HELP WANTED', he would run across the road, dodging in and out of the carriages, knowing that jobs could go as soon as they were advertised. And then, at the bottom of the sign he had to read the words in smaller print, 'No Irish Need Apply.'

He sometimes earned 10 cents for carrying someone's bag or holding a horse for an hour while a gentleman went to his bank. But that was just enough to buy Eamonn a bite to eat so he didn't have to break into the money they had brought with them from Ireland. He would need all their money to rent a room, and he needed even more money to send for his mother and brothers as well as to feed them all when they came. He needed work, a proper job, not just enough to keep him alive.

There were plenty of people who needed to beg. But Eamonn remembered his father's anger at the idea they should beg for food from Kate's grandfather. He had had enough of begging. All he wanted was work. At houses where they were looking for boys to do the dirty jobs, he would arrive at the back door and say to the cook or the butler, 'I'm sorry. I'm Irish, but I'm good at cleaning.' But soon he had had enough of saying, 'I'm sorry, I'm Irish.'

There were men he heard talking about the Gold Rush, drunken men sitting beside the river swearing that if only they had the money to go out west they'd join an expedition, Indians or no Indians. And Eamonn used to sit beside his tree when no one was around, counting the last of their money and working out that it would be just enough to carry him across to Texas or Arizona where there was supposed to be gold enough for everyone and millionaires made every day. But he didn't want to leave his family even further behind him. So he looked towards New York.

Everyone he asked in Boston said he'd been stupid to stop there and expect his aunt to help them when most people knew it was hard for the Irish to get work. New York was quite another thing, they said. The place was teeming with money, dripping with money. There were splendid hotels, all in need of boot boys, and hundreds of shops and offices, and all of them needed messenger boys, with no questions asked about who they were and where they came from.

When Eamonn asked the men and boys who met together by the river why none of them went to New York in search of the work they wanted, they were silent. They were silent until they started to tell their stories again—stories about the people from Ireland who had started off as messenger boys, and had made their fortune in America. There was only one man had anything bad to say about New York, but he had lived there ten years before.

Noah Wood, a man from England who said he used to work as a tailor before America ruined him, said that New York was so dirty and uncivilized that piglets ran around the streets like stray dogs and nobody cleared the dirt away. None of the others believed a word that Noah said and Eamonn could understand why they liked to live on the other stories, the stories of fine shops and fine hotels, because in those stories there were none of the notices Eamonn saw everywhere he turned in Boston.

NO IRISH NEED APPLY.

By the time the policeman woke him up and moved him along from his usual sleeping place, Eamonn was ready to move himself on again and try to find work in

New York. The policeman followed him as he walked towards the bridge.

'You're walking too slowly, youngster. Why aren't you heading off towards home?'

'I haven't got a home to go to.'

'What about your folks?'

'They got sick. They're still up there.' He motioned with his head. 'Near Quebec.'

The policeman whistled. 'So where were you going to sleep tonight?'

'Under the tree. Where I usually sleep. It's not cold.'

'And what are you going to do tomorrow?'

Eamonn straightened up proudly. 'Tomorrow I'm going to go to New York. You can get work there even if you're Irish. They don't mind.'

'There's work in Boston. You don't have to go all that way.'

Eamonn shook his head. 'NO IRISH NEED APPLY. Have you never seen that?'

Then the policeman told him of a cotton mill, on the edge of the town, run by an Irish man. 'Well, his father was Irish,' the policeman said, 'but he's done all right for himself. He won't turn Irish people away if there's work to be had.'

'Move your feet.' The little girl had to shout twice at Eamonn to make herself heard above the clatter and hiss of the machines and the loud singing of the girls and men working the looms.

'Move your feet, you great loon!'

The loud voice and the cursing came out of a thin little girl with a bleached white face. A few freckles over her nose were the only sign that she had ever been anywhere near the sun. But she had sun-golden hair, in hundreds of curls that shimmered in and out of the unbleached fluff of the cotton. Annie O'Dwyer was seven, the same age as

73

Shaun but as old as the hills, crawling in and out under the looms and knotting up the broken threads or helping to thread the warp before they started on another weaving.

Eamonn never saw her with shoes on, so her bare feet were always covered in oil and coated in the fibres flying around everywhere. She always wore a green checked pinafore over her flowered dress, and on top of everything she wore a smile. Even when she was yelling at the other workers who were in her way, her bright, white teeth flashed into a smile.

'Move your feet, I said. Where were you born? In a haystack?'

Eamonn had been miles away in his thoughts. Whatever he was doing, working with his hands, his thoughts were always miles away. In his dreams and when he was awake he retraced his steps, back to Buchanans' house and then back to Grosse Isle to where he had left his mother still sick and where he had lost his brothers. They were his reason for working from six in the morning until six at night, when the night shift took over. And if they had let him he would have worked through the night as well as long as he could at the mill, to let him save money faster and be with his family.

He didn't sit down and count his money too often. Ever since he had got his job at the Kerry Mills he had rented a bed in a room near the mill. He carried his money with him all the time because another boy, a boy who did the night shifts, had the use of his bed during the day. But he didn't bother himself too much with counting the money. It was going to take him years to save up enough to bring his family down to be with him. And perhaps they would have forgotten him by then. Shaun might even have forgotten him already.

Annie O'Dwyer had forgotten everything about her family. When he asked her where she came from, she said, 'Don't know.' Only a few words she spoke gave away that she came from Galway where Eamonn's family had lived until the landlords and hunger drove them out.

Annie stayed in the house next to Eamonn's and took it upon herself to arrive and yell in his ear in the mornings as soon as she found out where he was sleeping. 'Get up, you lazy loon! You don't want your pay docking just for a minute's late.' And they ran through the streets together, dodging the dirt and the drunkards holding out their hands for money. One morning, Eamonn asked Annie what had happened to her father and mother. 'Did the fever take them?'

'Don't know.' Annie grinned. 'Don't know nothing.'

He asked the other workers in the mill, but all they knew was that she'd been working there a year, she hadn't grown an inch and probably never would and she'd been brought there for work by the woman whose house she lived in. There were plenty of little ones like her, running about under the machines collecting the lint and tying up threads, all the work that only they could do because they were small enough to get under there and their hands were thin enough to thread the warp.

One Thursday evening near the end of their shift, Eamonn was lost again in his usual daydreams. His hands worked away automatically at scattering the cotton over the carding machine. He had stopped noticing the searing, stinging smell of the ammonia from the chemical room so that his hands rose automatically to wipe the tears from his eyes without him realizing that they were stinging and red. He had counted his money in his head and counted up how much he would earn in the next three months. And he had gone over again his own long, cold journey from Quebec as far as St John and his incredible good fortune at getting his railway ticket paid for him. He couldn't hope for that for his mother and brothers, but he had to get the money somehow. His life would never be right until he got his family all together again. A part of him, a part of his soul, was still back there with them. He would have to get some work in the evening, perhaps not the whole of the night. But he had to find some way to sleep less and earn a few more cents.

There was a scream. Eamonn jumped up and leaped sideways into the narrow aisle between his row of machines and the next. The machines carried on, clattering above the noise of the screaming, like a steam engine that takes hundreds of yards to come to a halt. A child was under the machines. Golden hair flashed among the fluff of the unbleached cotton. The machines stopped and then there was just crying and a loud child's voice shouting and crying.

'Where've you been sleeping? Get me out of here.'

Annie was caught by her long curls under the machine. Another few seconds and her hair would have ripped and pulled her right in. She had blood pouring from a cut behind her ear, but it was Eamonn who fainted, felt sick, and thudded to the floor.

When he came round there was the sound of thick, coarse cloth-cutting scissors hacking at Annie's hair and she was yelling at them, 'Leave off. Leave me some hair, will you?' But none of her curls were left. She was shorn like a boy all ready for the summer's heat and they sent her home with a huge piece of cotton bound tightly round her head.

'Did it hurt a lot?' Eamonn asked.

'Dunno.' Annie held his hand and they didn't run back to their lodgings as they usually did, keen to find out if there was anything left for them to eat or whether they would first have to go out and buy their food. 'I just want to know who dunnit. Who left that machine lock open? That's what I want to know.'

Eamonn felt sick again. She could have been killed. He was going to make sure his brothers never had to do that sort of work, or any sort of work until they'd had a good education.

That night he dreamed of Shaun being caught on the spikes of the carding machine and dreamt that he shouted out, 'No! He's not meant to be working here. Why isn't he at school? I thought he was doing his lessons.' Then he woke up calling out, 'No!' and the boy in the next bed shouted at him, 'Leave off, will you. It isn't time to get up yet.' Eamonn had no idea what time it was. In the dark cellar where they were sleeping there was never light to tell them the time of day. Annie was the one who woke them up on time.

The next day she was there just as usual, still with the piece of cotton bandaged round her head and her shorn hair making her look like a boy. Her face was streaked with dirt and tears.

'You need a wash, Annie.'

'You need a wash yourself.'

'I put my head under the pump last night at least.'

'Well, I didn't. I went to sleep. All right? I got to sleep sometime.'

Eamonn took her hand. She was only as old as Shaun. From behind, when you looked at her skinny legs and her dirty bare feet she was a good deal smaller than Shaun and looked three years younger. But when you looked in her face there was a something about her much older and tougher that said, 'I can take care of myself.'

'Is your head hurting?'

'Dunno.' Annie coughed. The way to work was quiet and slow and they only just got to the door before the hooter sounded. All that day, Eamonn kept his eye on her as much as he could, but it was hard to find her most of the time as she darted in and out of the different rooms, under machines and hidden behind people's elbows.

On the way home, Eamonn held Annie's hand again. They stopped at the beginning of their alleyway, while a rat-poison man trickled turquoise green liquid along the lane in the cracks of all the cobbles.

'How's your head?' Eamonn asked.

Annie raised her right foot and stepped carefully onto the first cobble, trying to avoid the cracks between the cobbles with their sparkling turquoise streams of poison. 'Dunno. Why? Why d'you keep on asking?'

'You're like my little sister, now,' said Eamonn. 'I have to look after you. Someone has to.'

'I can look after myself.' Annie stood on a cobble island in the middle of the glittering, greeny-turquoise poison, looking round for the next safe place to put her bare feet. 'But I can be like your sister, if you want. I never had no brothers. As far as I know.'

They hung around the streets together in the evenings after that, as long as the light held, because neither of them wanted to turn in before they needed to and sleep in their dark cellars. Eamonn wanted to take Annie to the places he had first been in Boston, to the tree by the river where he had slept for the first two months. But it was all too far away for them to get to in an evening. The only place they ever went apart from work was church on Sunday, where there was sometimes cake and tea.

It was Father Grogan who gave Eamonn some paper and let him use a table in his office to write. Annie sat beside him, biting her lips and staring at the signs he made on paper. 'I'm going to do that too,' she said. 'And when I can write, then I can write letters.'

While Eamonn tried to concentrate on writing to his mother, Annie kept on interrupting him, 'Who shall I write to, Eamonn?'

He shook his head, 'Dunno.' But after he had finished he started trying to teach her how to read and write. She liked to hear him read, from the New Testaments there were in the priest's house, and she liked it in the evenings when Eamonn told her stories he remembered, but there were no story books to read like the story books they'd had at Kate's house back in Tullamore.

Annie wouldn't have been able to read them anyway. She was hopeless. Eamonn would put her finger on the print and read along the line as he read aloud. Then Annie would read back to him what he had just said. She had a good memory. She could remember whole sentences at a time that he had read to her. But if he pointed to a word he thought she had just learned, and asked her to read it back to him from another page, she couldn't.

One day she said, 'I think I could just about read, Eamonn. But how do you stop those little black things from dancing around on the page?'

He sighed. 'I think you need glasses, Annie.'

'Never. You'll never get me wearing glasses.'

There was no reply to the letters Eamonn wrote to Grosse Isle. He had written asking how his mother was and where he could get in touch with his brothers, but there was no reply. In the end, he wrote to the priest at Buchanans' church and asked if he could help to find them all. He waited for a month or more and nothing came. He asked Father Grogan to try and find out what had happened to his aunt, Mary Kennedy, but there was no news there either.

Sometimes, when Eamonn sat down to write a letter to his mother, knowing that there would be no reply, he remembered the letter he ought to have written to Kate and her family in Tullamore.

He had promised to write and let them know as soon as he and his family arrived safely in America. But he had put his letter off until he earned his first good wage and could start to think of paying Kate back all the money she had given them to make the journey. Then the journey had taken so long and the quarantine had held them up for months. How could he write to Kate now, when he had lost them all and he was the only one who had actually made it to America. He wasn't going to write with such terrible news. The letter would have to wait.

He had to find his family first and look after them. For the moment, the best he could do was to look after Annie.

NINE

'That's not the point.' Joe Brady scrubbed across his face with the sleeve of his jacket and smeared it even dirtier with sweat and smoke and tears. 'There were too many of them working in that room. Even the smell of that stuff could have killed them. Not just the fire. That's why they jumped. It was the smells choking them.'

Gresham's Mills didn't have anything to do with Eamonn or Joe. It was one of the three mills across in the next street. The owner was an American, but most of the workers there were Irish. So when the fire had started their boss had sent for the men and boys from Kerry Mills, where Eamonn and Joe and Annie worked, to help with hauling water for the fire brigade.

'They shouldn't have been using candles.'

One of the older men stood with his back against the gateway to a brewery across the street. There was nothing more they could do, now the fire was out. Gresham's workers had all gone home and the firemen were sorting through the smouldering ruins. Eamonn and all the others had lost a day's pay for being outside and the boss hadn't called them back to work.

Joe Brady, a boy a year or two older than Eamonn, lit up a cigarette. 'That's not the point, how the fire started,' Joe said. 'There were too many people crammed in there. In that one room, doing all the things they do in the bigger mills. They were lucky no one got killed.'

He was fifteen years old and his white forehead, blackened by the smoke, was wrinkled like that of an old man. He screwed his eyes up and took a long drag at his cigarette.

'It wouldn't have happened, though. Not if they hadn't

had candles. That's what I say. The boss won't allow candles near our chemicals room.'

A crowd of tiny children came and went near the burnt-out gates of the factory, trying to get a look at what had happened and being chased away by the men who had been working to put out the blaze.

'I used to work there,' Brady said at last. 'He used to get mad at us for going to the door to snatch a breath of fresh air. So he locked the door. We had to work with the door locked and you couldn't hardly breathe in there. That's the point.' He wiped his sleeve across his eyes again. 'When that fire started, they were all locked in. That's the point. That's why they were jumping out the window, screaming, and him standing out here and telling us to be careful not to drench his machinery. It makes you sick. They could have all been killed, and him telling us not to drench his machines.'

He sat down on the ground and put his head between his knees.

There was no point. There was no sense in any of it.

Eamonn sat down next to Joe, putting an arm around his shoulders. The older man across the narrow alleyway nodded at Joe. 'A lot of his friends were in there. It's the shock. And some of them are in a bad way after jumping out of the windows, like.'

He strolled over towards them and talked about Joe as if he wasn't there. 'He got the sack from Gresham's when he made a fuss. The owner said he was a troublemaker.' He prised Joe's cigarette out of his clenched fingers and took a drag from it himself. 'Gresham said he'd see Joe never worked again. But he got another job all right. He's a good, strong worker. And maybe none of us would have worked if they'd stopped him from working.'

Eamonn's shirt sleeves were too wet from the hoses to wipe Joe's tears, so he stroked his head and shoulders.

'You talk a load of nonsense,' he said. 'You couldn't afford to stop work if they threw Joe here out. You couldn't afford to give up your jobs as well. What would you all do without work?'

The man shifted his weight from one foot to the other. He took a long time to answer, and looked into Eamonn's eyes as if he was trying to read what Eamonn was thinking.

'You're right,' he said. 'We couldn't manage without the bit of money from our work. But think about it. How would they manage if they didn't have us to do their jobs for them?'

Eamonn knew the answer to that one. There were people enough out there who'd be ready to do the work if the old man and Joe Brady and everyone else in the Kerry Mills decided they wouldn't work. The old man must be soft in the head.

Joe wiped his eyes and sat staring across at the burned out building. His eyes followed the length of the fence, over the broken-down gates, and scanned the walls and the broken windows that had burst outwards with the heat. Then he stood up and walked from one end of the wall to the other. At three places along the wall he rubbed the soot away with his jacket sleeve. Then he pointed up to a space in the charred, wooden wall between two windows on the second floor. The letters K and N were still visible, daubed in red paint. Brady showed Eamonn and the old man the same letters in the three places where he had rubbed the soot away.

'What does that stand for?'

Eamonn went up close to one of the daubs of red paint, on the fence that had once been green, and traced the letters with his fingers.

The old man from Kerry Mills closed his right eye and made an O shape over his nose out of his thumb and first finger.

'I Knows Nothing,' Brady said. 'The Know-Nothings. They want America for the Americans and they want the Irish out.'

82

'They didn't start the fire?'

Eamonn's flattened hand covered up the filthy red letters, as if covering them up could erase them from the building and make time run backwards to stop the fire.

'They wouldn't try to kill people?'

'They've killed people already. Why should they stop now?'

'But why kill us?' Eamonn took his hand off the wall and tried to get rid of the dirt and red paint by rubbing both of his hands together. But the dirt from the fire clung to his hands and his clothes. 'You mean they want to kill us just because we're Irish?'

Joe took a drag on his cigarette, coughed and stubbed it out, carefully putting the stub in his pocket. 'You don't know much, do you, Kennedy?'

Eamonn was all for telling the police about the letters on the wall, but Joe shrugged his shoulders. 'What do you think they'll do?'

'The police were here too, helping us to put out the fire. They'll want to know who started it.'

'Don't you think they saw the letters? You don't know the half of it, do you, Kennedy? Some of the police belong to the Know-Nothings. Maybe all of the police. They don't want Irish taking their jobs.'

Eamonn had to run to keep up with Joe, who took great long strides whenever he was angry about something.

'But we don't take their jobs, Joe. We're not trying to be policemen.'

'They don't want the Irish taking any jobs. They want us put on ships and sent back to where we came from. Where do you come from, Kennedy?'

Eamonn sighed. 'We've come a long way from Galway and we lived in Tullamore.'

Joe stopped and turned round.

'I'll tell you what, Kennedy. My folks would like you. Do you want to live in my house? Our mammy is out all day at the cleaning, but she won't mind if you stay. And she won't mind if you come from Galway.'

'I can't leave Annie.'

'Who's Annie?'

'You know, the loud one with the blonde curls, the little girl who shouts a lot. She's like my sister. I look after her.'

'She can come too.'

Eamonn crept along behind Joe Brady, clutching Annie's hand. Her landlady had made a fuss when they said she was going to leave and Joe had had to deal with her.

'I've looked after that child like a mother,' she said. And then Joe had asked her where Annie's wages had gone. 'I've been looking after her money for her,' the landlady said. 'She's too small a one to look after money all by herself.'

'Well, we'll look after it now.' Joe held out his hand. 'Annie's coming to live with us and she needs her money.'

'I don't have all of it just at this moment,' the woman said. 'And I had to use some of it to pay for her room and her food. There won't be much left, when you think of all the food she's eaten. It's the small ones as eats the most, you know. You'd never think such a small child could eat so much.'

Eamonn knew that Annie never got enough to eat because of all the times he'd bought her an apple or a hot potato when he met her outside her house after she was supposed to have eaten her evening meal. But Joe didn't stop to argue. 'We'll come back for the rest tomorrow,' he said.

When they went back the next day, to get Annie's money, the woman wasn't there any more. A woman who looked near enough like her to be her sister told them the landlady had moved out and no one knew where she had gone.

After that, Annie could save at least some of her money, even after she had paid the Bradys for food. Staying in the Brady family's three rooms meant that Eamonn could save another few cents a week as well. Annie slept in one room with Brady's four sisters and Eamonn slept on a mattress in the other room with the boys. Mr and Mrs Brady slept in the kitchen, when they weren't in the middle of cooking for all the children they'd gathered around them. When their son brought home two more children for them they just smiled.

'It's like a madhouse here,' Mr Brady said, 'a regular bedlam. Stay as long as you like.'

And there, in amongst the noise of seven children, the jumping around and scolding and chasing and gossip and stories and laughter, Eamonn found peace and quiet and felt protected for the first time since he had left Grosse Isle. He listened to Joe's talks with his father. After the fire at Gresham's Mills he learned all about groups like the faceless Know-Nothings, working to get the Irish thrown out of America. And still he felt safe. He and Annie were safe and warm with enough to eat and jobs where they earned enough for him to save. He felt safe enough to dream of the time when he could go and look for his brothers again.

Mr Brady looked smaller than his wife. It was the way he moved that made you think of him as small. He was thin and energetic, with a smile on his face like a leprechaun who knows he's never going to lose his pot of gold, darting about from one child to another, grabbing their faces and giving them a wash that was no more than a splash with a cloth, or wiping the dishes and throwing them up to a wooden plate rack. He told stories too, and pulled his rubber face into gargoyle grimaces every night when the littlest Bradys and then Annie demanded his story about the Wide-Mouthed Toad.

Mrs Brady was hard at work cleaning all day and Mr Brady was always home before her, because Kerry Mills was closer. So he was the one to scrub the potatoes and set them on to cook before his wife got home.

One day, a month after Eamonn and Annie moved in, he was putting the huge, heavy pot on to boil when Eamonn and Annie and Joe strolled in. Eamonn was scared.

'Mr Brady, I've seen two men making the Know-Nothing sign, at the corner of Paradise Street. Are they going to start a fire? Shall we tell the police?'

Mr Brady threw a good bit of salt into the pot and shook his head.

'No. The police're no good. We'll have to get our people out.'

Joe nodded at his father and went out again.

'What are we going to do?'

'I'm going to cook the dinner first. You can't do anything without food inside you. And you're going to take the little ones to the pump and scrub their hands and faces. We're all off to church after that, so I want them faces clean. It's the church they'll go for.'

He put the lid on the pot. 'I don't think much of them bishops, but we can't let people get beaten up, just because they're Catholic and Irish. We've got to get up there and keep that lot out of the church.'

Eamonn never found out how Mr Brady knew who would be the next target of the Know-Nothings. But he was right about the church. He was always right.

It was quiet when they walked inside St Patrick's Church, dark and quiet, but lit by a hundred candles or more from the hundred people already sitting there, some of them whispering rosaries, others staring at the altar.

Mr Brady walked to the front and spoke to the priest. There was a burst of a whispered argument and then the priest raised his arms and spoke.

'Mr Brady thinks . . . ' He paused and the crowd of people already in the church started to chatter more loudly until the priest carried on, 'We cannot sit here and be led like lambs to the slaughter. Mr Brady thinks we should go out to meet them.'

There was a rustling of applause and then a voice from the back called out, 'And what do you think, Father?'

'I think Mr Brady's right. This is our church. The militiamen are coming. They've promised us protection. But it's time we showed those troublemakers we can stand up for ourselves.'

There was a cheer and people started heading to the great church doors, men and women, with children to stay inside. Joe and Eamonn didn't count as children and Annie slipped out anyway. Together, all linking arms, they stood on the steps of the church and waited.

Eamonn had never seen the Know-Nothings. It was Joe who had pointed out the two rough men exchanging their secret sign. He thought then they would all look filthy and fierce. Instead of that, as they stood on the steps of St Patrick's, a line of well-dressed men approached, men in shining, tall, beaver hats and tailcoats, men wearing silk ties and embroidered waistcoats. Then came another line and then another, at least two hundred men, marching in formation like a proper army.

They could have gone back into the church then, and prayed. They could have sat and waited quietly for the militiamen to come.

But the people defending their church didn't wait for the attack. They had heard already of churches burning down, in Philadelphia and Pennsylvania. They had seen the mills where Irish people worked being destroyed and the miserable cellars where Irish people lived being boarded up. There were no great speeches. Nobody told them what to do. But the people inside the church and the others streaming to join them every minute knew what they had to do. And they were not going to let a troop of men in their fancy clothes force them back to Ireland to starve. Without any warning, Mrs Brady picked up a loose paving stone and threw it at the first line of men.

The row of top hats ducked and one fell off, and the crowd of people waiting on the steps cheered.

The wave of people surging forwards was an angry, storm-swollen river, bursting its banks. The men in top hats scattered, running back towards the bridge, turning to fight and then turning to run again as row after row of Irish mothers came at them and battered them with umbrellas and bags and anything else they had to hand. And in the end it was Mrs Brady and four of her friends who finished them off and sent the last ones fleeing away, hopping and running in all directions, by grabbing hold of one of the smaller men and flinging him over the parapet of the bridge into the river, where they stood laughing as he first went under and then swam away.

As the last few top hats disappeared, the little ones rushed to the church door and had the extra pleasure of seeing the militiamen arrive too late, with bayonets fixed and uniforms polished bright enough to blind anyone who dared to step out against them.

After all the excitement was over and the church was locked up and all of their friends had shaken hands and been hugged, Mr Brady and Eamonn and Joe strode in triumph along the middle of the road towards their house, each with a little one perched on their shoulders. And Mr Brady said they would all by now have been burned alive if they had decided to wait for the military.

'That lot couldn't have hurt us!' Mrs Brady said. 'All them silly little men in hats. Such cowards, they were. Did you see them run?'

'If we'd stayed in that church and waited,' Mr Brady smiled at the little ones, 'believe me, they would have done what they came to do. And they would have had what they've always wanted—Roasted Catholic and Jesuit Soup.'

'What's in a Jesuit Soup?' said Annie.

TEN

Mr Brady worked in a different part of the mill to Eamonn and Annie and Joe. He was a machine operator and brought home a deal more money. He never saw what happened in the other parts of the works, but he questioned Joe and Eamonn about their work every night. They were clever lads, he used to say, and should make it to foreman one day.

So Joe didn't tell his father. It was Eamonn who had to tell him about the trouble Joe got himself into, with the foreman.

Joe and Eamonn had been busy working on the same carding machine when the foreman asked Annie to run under the machine and clear a blockage.

'Joe told him he shouldn't make her do that unless the machinery was switched off,' Eamonn said. 'But the foreman wouldn't listen to him. He just got mad and went red in the face. He said if we switched it off, we'd need four minutes to get it started again. He just shoved Joe out of the way and turned to Annie and said, "Come on, little 'un. I'm relying on you to clear the grids."'

'Where's Joe now?' Mr Brady picked up one of the big metal buckets they took to the pump and tipped water out of it into a bowl. Eamonn stepped back. He didn't want to get Joe into trouble. He had never seen Mr Brady angry before, or hit anyone, but he looked angry enough to hit someone now.

'I don't think Joe meant any wrong.'

Mr Brady was scrubbing the porridge plates left over from breakfast.

'I don't think. I know he didn't mean any wrong. He's not the sort to do anything wrong, my son. He'd do what he thought was fair.'

Eamonn tried again. 'Joe put his arm out to stop Annie bending her head and nipping under the machine, and he shouted at the foreman. He had to shout because the machine was too loud. He shouted, "We have to switch the machine off. It says so in the rules."'

'That's right.' Mr Brady dunked the next plate in the cold water, and the next, pushing them down as if he was holding someone down to drown them. 'You've got to look after the safety. With them big machines. He did right.'

'But the foreman got really mad and grabbed hold of Annie's other arm and said, "There isn't time. She's getting on with her work. It's me the bosses'll shout at if we don't get finished in time. Now get down there and get cleared up." And he gave Annie a kind of shove. And then . . .'

Eamonn took the first of the plates off Mr Brady and shook the drops of water at the little ones sitting on the floor, so that they jumped and laughed and ran away. 'Annie turned around and made as if to go under the rope. But I didn't want her to go, so I told her not to as well. You've seen that cut over by her ear where she got caught that time and they had to cut off all her hair. Then Joe stopped his work altogether and grabbed hold of Annie and just sat down on the floor, with her sitting down on his knee, his arms holding her tight so she wouldn't run and do the job in spite of him. She's that wilful. It all went dead quiet. Nobody was singing. Nobody was talking. There was just the noise of the machines going on and on. And people were making out they were still working, and they were. But they were watching as well. Everyone was watching.'

There wasn't much more to tell. The plates were washed and the potatoes were put on to boil and by the time Mrs Brady got home from her long trek across Boston after her cleaning work, Eamonn had got near the end of his story.

'Just when Joe sat down with Annie on his lap, holding her tight so she wouldn't run off and nip inside the machine while it was still running, one of the bosses walked in, another Mr Doyle it was.'

There were plenty of Mr Doyles in Boston. The owner of the Kerry Mills was probably just as nice as anyone else when he was at home with his family or out for a walk in the park. At his mill all he thought about was time and money. And everyone knew that time was money. Any time they weren't working was time when his mills were not making money.

Mrs Brady hung her shawl up on the hook by the back door and Eamonn carried on.

'The foreman told Mr Doyle that Joe had tried to stop Annie doing the work he'd asked her to. Mr Doyle listened to the foreman, but he wouldn't listen to anything Joe said, about safety or turning off the machines. Then he made us turn all the machines off. He said he had something important to say to all of his workers.

'He stood near the door of the weaving shed, with all the workers standing in front of him. We had to stand up straight like an army on parade because he shouted at us and told us to stand up straight and not slouch. Then he spoke like a priest in church and told us how we had an important job to do together, for America, to make our country prosperous. I thought he was going to say it was right to stop Annie going in under the machines, to keep her safe.'

Eamonn stood there, with the same plate and the same cloth he had been holding since he started his story.

'But then he started shouting. He shouted so's his voice hit the back of the hall and bounced back again. Annie had her fingers in her ears and Joe had his hands round her head so no one would see what she was up to. I don't think Mr Doyle would've noticed anyway. He just kept on shouting.

'And he got more and more angry. "Let me say this, once and for all," he said. He slammed his fist down hard on that counter next to the door. "No one is going to stop one of *my* workers from doing their job, the job I pay them well for. Anyone who tries to stop one of *my* workers from doing his job is no longer one of my workers."'

Mr Brady was sitting on the kitchen floor as Eamonn reached the end of his story. Mrs Brady stood in the doorway, with the four year old already perched in her arms, and listened quietly.

'And what did our Joe do then?' Mr Brady grinned. 'Don't tell me. He's lost his job, hasn't he? Old Doyle gave him the sack.'

Eamonn shook his head.

'Joe just stood up. He'd been sitting down the whole time, with Annie on his lap. Well, he stood up and he held on tight to her hand and he said, "I've never been one of *your* workers. I don't belong to you. I belong to myself." Mr Doyle put his arm up to stop them going out the door, so Joe ducked under Mr Doyle's arm and him and Annie just walked out.'

Eamonn didn't know what to make of the way Mr Brady kept on smiling. Joe might never work again, if the mill-owners round about knew he was a troublemaker. The family needed his money. And there was Annie's money as well. She didn't earn very much. But at least it paid for her food.

Mr Brady stood up and took the little boy from his wife. 'You get your shoes off and sit you down,' he said. 'You look worn out.' And then he grinned again, the four year old grinning too as he peered at his father from his cosy perch on Mr Brady's hip.

'Oh, I'd love to have seen old Doyley's face when our Joe told him what to do with his job. Where's the rascal now?'

'Mr Doyle went back to his office.'

'No, I meant Joe. Where's that rascal hiding himself?'

Eamonn shrugged his shoulders. 'I thought he would be here when I got home.'

'So what did the rest of you do, after all that fuss?'

'Mr Doyle told them to switch on the machines again and we all kept on working. Nobody talked very much. We were all too afraid of losing our jobs.'

'He was right, though,' Mr Brady said. 'He was right to stop Annie going in under the carding machine. There are too many people getting themselves hurt.'

Then he put the little boy down on the floor and shooed all the children outside to play.

Eamonn walked over to where the potatoes were bubbling away and poked at them with a fork.

'Maybe he wouldn't have lost his job if he hadn't spoken to Mr Doyle like that.'

Mr Brady sighed. 'I'm going to have to go and talk with the boss tomorrow and say we're sorry. And see if he'll give Joe and Annie their jobs back. What do you think?'

His wife looked angry. 'Joe did the right thing. They can't go around letting children get hurt. Annie's just a child. But Doyle couldn't care less if she gets killed in his machines. Joe was right.'

Mr Brady shook his head. 'I know all that. But Joe needs a job.' He clapped his hands together. 'I'll talk to Mr Doyle tomorrow and make things right.'

Joe had taken Annie to watch the ducks in a park he had once discovered a good three miles away. Annie had never been in a park before and couldn't remember the countryside she had left behind in Ireland. Joe had been teaching her to turn cartwheels in the park and then taught her to whistle all the way home.

The whistling got on Mrs Brady's nerves. 'A whistling woman and a crowing hen, would drive the devil out of his den,' she yelled at them and she sent them all out into the streets to play until very late that night.

Mr Brady didn't manage to get his son's job back.

Mr Doyle said, 'I can do without troublemakers here. Whole families of troublemakers.' And he told Mr Brady not to bother turning in to work again. 'I said yesterday that anyone who tries to stop one of my workers doing his job is not one of my workers any more. And I meant it. I can't trust a man who wants to bring troublemakers back in here.'

After that, Eamonn was the only one with a job. And Mrs Brady, who went out early every morning to clean and came back late at night, long after the mill shift had changed over. But Mr Brady was never idle.

That night there were visitors in their cellar kitchen, men from the mill with some of their wives. There were some who Eamonn didn't know, men who worked in the second building where Mr Brady had his work. But he recognized the old man who had been there helping them to put out the fire at Gresham's Mill. He remembered what the old man had said to him as well. He had been talking about the mill-owners and the way they treated their workers and he had watched Eamonn carefully, stared at him a long time before he said, 'How would the bosses manage if they didn't have us to do their jobs for them?'

That's what they talked about at Brady's house that night. It was the only thing they talked about. One or two of the men who didn't know Eamonn stopped in mid-sentence and stared at him when he walked into the room, but Mr Brady nodded at him. 'He's all right. He knows what's up at Kerry Mills.' And they went on talking, way into the night. The children fell asleep, sitting on visitors' laps, and had to be carried into the two bedrooms.

At daybreak Mrs Brady put her bonnet on and crept up the stairs. She hadn't slept a wink, but she had to go to work. She shook hands with all the visiting men and whispered, 'We'll work to keep you fed if you go on strike. Something has to be done.' And the other women nodded.

Eamonn hadn't slept all night either. In another hour he would have to set off for work at the mill, knowing that he was the only one left who could help to keep the family fed. He had his savings to help them as well, but the small amount he had managed to save, to bring his mother and brothers down to Boston, wouldn't go very far if Mr Brady and his son went without work for long.

'What about you, Eamonn?' Mr Brady closed the latch quietly after his wife had gone. 'Are you going to join us, lad? Join the union and join the strike?'

'I can't!' Eamonn rubbed his eyes.

Several times he had half dozed off and then jumped up and walked outside to wake himself up. The meeting was important enough to keep awake. He had never seen men and women get together like this, never heard the ideas they were putting forward.

Back home in Ballinglas, when his whole village had been tumbled, the houses razed to the ground and the people turned onto the streets, he had wanted to kill the landlord and the soldiers who had turned them out. But in the end nothing had been done. And the crowds of people, whole families, old and young, had just disappeared, spread out along the country roads and disappeared, too scared of what the soldiers with their guns could do, too frightened to fight back.

Now he was listening to talk of a different kind of fighting. Not fighting with guns. They could never win that way. They had no weapons and there had been enough killing. That was what they were trying to stop, people dying of hunger, people dying because nobody thought to protect them from the machines, people dying because they wanted to work and no one would give them a job. Now they were talking of fighting by simply not working.

'How would they manage, the bosses, if we weren't there to do their work for them?'

But someone had to go out to work. Someone had to get food for the family. And the Bradys wouldn't let their little children work. They couldn't stop Annie, once she had started. But the others were sent to a school for some of the time. There was no money coming in. Someone had to work.

'I can't strike,' Eamonn said. 'We would all starve. Someone's got to work.'

'That's just what we need to strike for,' Mr Brady said. 'We've all got to work. We want to make sure they don't throw people out of work for speaking up about things. Joe didn't do anything wrong. It was right to say Annie shouldn't go under machines with those great teeth whirring around her. It was right to speak out. And it's wrong for people to lose their jobs if they speak out. This is supposed to be a free country. Things are supposed to be better here than they were back home. Well, not if they're going to throw us out on the streets and leave us to starve, they aren't.'

'But what if I lose my job as well? What will we do? I slept outside in Boston in the spring. But it gets colder soon, and the little ones can't sleep outside. Let me keep on working. Then at least we'll have a bit to eat.'

'That's what they want. That's how they'll beat us, Eamonn. They want people who are so desperate that they'll put up with anything as long as they can have a job and a bite to eat. Well, they won't play that game with us. Not any longer.'

Mr Brady showed Eamonn a long, black book with a red binding, its pages neatly handwritten with rows of names and dates and figures.

'Everyone who joins the union pays as much as they can afford every week and we write it all down here. We keep the money safe, so if there has to be a strike we can help people out. It's all here, Eamonn. Nobody should have to work for a boss that's not treating his workers right—as long as we've got the union.' He flicked through the pages of the black and red book and showed Eamonn the sum of money getting larger and larger.

'We've got enough money to feed every union family in Kerry Mills for three weeks. And even after that, the other unions might be able to help us out. We can hold out for three weeks, Eamonn! Three weeks and more! Let's just see how well they manage without us to do their work for three weeks.'

Eamonn was scared. For the first time in two years he had felt he belonged somewhere. He had a job and a place to live, with a family who made him welcome and were keen to make his family welcome as soon as he could get them to Boston. Eamonn knew it would take him a few years to get all his family back together at the rate he was able to save money, but at least he had made a start. And that wasn't counting the money his mother might be earning once she got better. For the first time in two years, Eamonn had had a few months of going forwards. And now the steady ground he had built his hopes on was slipping away again. He was scared.

He was scared of having to sleep out in the open again. The whole Brady family would be thrown out onto the streets. He was scared of having to walk miles, begging for work as he had done until the job at Kerry Mills had turned up. And most of all he was scared of going hungry, of watching the little Brady children and Annie cry and then go quiet because they were too hungry and too tired to cry. He knew what it was like to watch people die of hunger. And he remembered the disease that followed up the hunger, kicking the people who were already half dead, finishing off the job.

He was scared of the way Mr Brady ignored all that. It was as if he didn't realize what could happen. Eamonn knew he would never have told people to give up their jobs if ever he had had to watch his own children go hungry for days on end. You had to make sure you had enough to eat before you could think about arguing with the bosses. But Mr Brady didn't seem worried about food or anything else. He said they would go ahead with the strike.

Eamonn said nothing. There was nothing he could do. If he went on strike, he was betraying his family, losing the money he had saved to get his mother and brothers back together again. If he went to work, he was betraying the men, women, and children all around him in Boston, the people who had helped him. He wanted to fight someone, the enemy, not his family or his friends. But he couldn't see the enemy. They said the strike was the only way to fight, but agreeing to go on strike with them was worse, much worse, than the day he had set out to cross the Atlantic in an ancient, broken-down ship. Then he had believed that all the hardship would be worth it in the end, that landing in America would make up for anything they suffered on the journey. Now, he believed the strike was a ship steering straight for dangerous rocks.

On the first day, Eamonn and the Bradys walked to the mill at the usual time. But instead of going inside, they waited across the road and had a word with everyone who was just about to go in the gates. There were some who pleaded that they had to work so their families wouldn't go hungry. To them, Mr Brady promised help with food. Others told him they were afraid to lose their jobs and he persuaded them that they were striking so a boss couldn't just take your job away for no reason.

Some people talked for a long time with Mr Brady or one of the other men and then said sadly that they couldn't manage without the money and walked in through the gates. One of the strikers started to swear at the first man who went through the gates, but Mr Brady put his hand out and covered the man's mouth.

'Least said, soonest mended, my lad,' he said. 'You might be working with that man on the next machine in a day or two.'

Nobody walked right past them without stopping to talk about the strike. Everyone said that Joe had done the right thing when he stopped Annie from going in under the machine. By the end of the first day, only six people had gone into the factory. They left by the back gate, the factory stayed quiet and the gates were closed. Mr Brady and his friends were sure they had won. That night more visitors piled into the Brady's cellar kitchen, taking a drop to drink and swapping stories of what had happened during the day.

There was even a visitor from another mill, where they had been on strike the year before. They hadn't won the strike, but in the end most of them had got their jobs back. He had come to tell them what to do.

'Be prepared for a long run,' he said. 'You'll have to set up a soup kitchen and make sure people don't get used to eating too much. They're bound to try to starve you out.'

Mr Brady kept on smiling. 'They won't have a single worker tomorrow. They can't hold out that long.'

The union man shrugged his shoulders.

'They might decide to just call this their annual shut-down, like holiday time, when none of you gets paid anyway.'

On the second day, two notices appeared on the mill gates. One said that anyone who had had anything to do with the strike was dismissed. The other notice advertised for expert mill workers and offered 1 cent more a day than any of the workers had been getting so far. People came from a long way away to ask about the jobs. They had seen the notices up in other parts of the city as well, and all of them were desperate for work.

Day after day, people turned up at the gates and checked the notices to see if they were in the right place before they went to ring the bell. And Mr Brady and his friends spoke to every one who came, telling them what had happened. They told them about children getting killed under the machines and said the same thing could happen again unless workers stood together. Very few newcomers walked past the line of men and women and tried for a job in the mills. The gates stayed closed and Mr Brady made speeches to the people on strike, urging them to stick together.

'United we stand. Divided we fall,' he said at the end of every speech and the crowds cheered him. But he started to look worried. Two weeks had gone by and still they were locked out of the mill and no one came out to talk to them.

Eamonn was angry with Mr Brady for making him go on strike, but he was scared to talk to him. So he tackled Joe's mother. She went outside to sweep the step one evening when the rooms were full of visitors and Eamonn offered to take the broom and do the job for her. But she wanted to stay outside in the fresh air.

'There's too much talking going on back there.' She gave the step a vigorous stab so that clouds of dust flew off the edge. 'A load of hot air, if you ask me. As if we didn't have enough to do.'

On Sundays, when she didn't have to go out cleaning, she had started to organize a soup kitchen. She reeled off the list of ingredients people had got through at the last evening serving and said, 'Mr Brady's got no idea what people can get through. He doesn't know what we have to do for the soup kitchen.'

'He's got no idea,' Eamonn agreed. 'He doesn't know what you've got to do for anything. He wouldn't have made us all go on strike and lose our money and lose our jobs if he had ever had to go hungry like my family.'

Mrs Brady leaned on her brush and smiled at him.

'My! Aren't we feeling sorry for ourselves today? What side of the bed did you get up out of? I thought you were all in favour of the strike and showing them who's in charge.'

Then she bent down and picked up the last traces of grit all stuck in the cracks in the step.

'And don't you go thinking Joe's father doesn't know what it is to go hungry. Now sit down there, now I've made a clean enough place for the Queen of England to sit down on. Sit down there and listen to me.'

Eamonn sat down on the step and Mrs Brady sat beside him and put her arm around him.

'Why do you think we came to Boston?'

Eamonn shifted to the right of the step and she took her arm away.

'It's because Mr Brady knows what it is to go hungry he's doing all this. We came all the way over here after seeing his brother and sister and their whole families wiped out with the sickness. He's not putting up with it no more. He's not going to sit by and let them treat the workers badly after we've come all this way, and them all boasting about how America is the land of the free where any man can make a fine living for his wife and his family if he's not afraid of work. Where did being good and keeping quiet and doing what you're told get us? Hmm?'

Eamonn picked up the handle of the stiff-bristled brush and swept away from where they were sitting, from the step almost to where the pavement met the road. 'But how much longer can it last?'

'I don't know. We'll hold out however long it takes. Or else they'll have their wives to answer to.'

At the beginning of the third week the militia were brought in, young, frightened-looking soldiers, with tall shiny hats strapped under their chins and bayonets fixed. They stood in a line along the road, aiming their weapons at the row of striking workers who had tried peacefully to persuade others not to break their strike. That day, a few new workers turned up. Mr Brady and the others were kept from talking to them by the soldiers who stood in front and backed them away from the mill towards the wall. But word had got round about their struggle and still there weren't enough workers from outside prepared to break the strike. The mills stayed quiet.

After the third week, fewer people came out to stand in the line and persuade the workers not to go back. There were meetings every night and people still came to those and the women were always out, gathering food wherever they could get it, making soup and porridge to feed the children. No one had to go hungry. But some started moaning about the money they couldn't send back to Ireland to their wives or their old parents back home.

'It's not just the children here we have to feed,' they grumbled at the meeting. 'There's my sister's children back in Dublin depending on me too.'

Then some started to say they ought to go back to work. The women were all against that, the women more than the men. They said the whole strike would be a waste if they went back to work without seeing the boss, without him making any promises about safe machines and safe jobs. The women got up and spoke at the meetings now, telling the strikers not to waste the fight. They said they would strangle their menfolk if anyone of them dared to think of going back.

Two of the families lost their rented rooms. The priest put them up in the church hall secretly because there was no money for rooms, only enough for food. But he wasn't sure how long he could let them stay. There were mill-owners using his church as well as the workers. Father Grogan would challenge the mill-owners to their faces and ask them if they really wanted to see fellow Catholics out on the streets—and them with five children too. But he knew that the bishop would interfere as soon as he found out the parish hall was being used to keep strikers.

The strike ended quietly.

Somebody said the bosses had promised to keep to the safety rules in future. They said all the workers could have their jobs back at the old rate, except for the Brady family.

The Bradys were troublemakers, the bosses said. And troublemakers would not be allowed back.

The other strikers wanted to stay out. They wanted to strike until the Bradys got their jobs back, but it was Mr Brady who said the strike was over. It had lasted nearly five weeks. The money was gone. He didn't want the union to be broken.

He walked proudly at the head of the workers as they walked back to work the next day. Then he stood outside the mill with Eamonn and Annie and Joe until the hooter started and the great gates shut.

'Has anyone ever won against the bosses?'

It was the first time Eamonn had dared to ask that question.

'Not yet.' Mr Brady took one of Annie's hands and his son took hold of the other and they swung her along between them. 'But that's no reason for giving up. We won on one thing. They've said they'll watch the machine safety. And they know that if they ask anyone in there now to send a child under a working machine again, they'll have another strike on their hands. There's some things you have to put up with and some things you don't. We don't have to put up with them killing children, just so their machines don't lose any time.'

And he counted to three and gave Annie another great leap through the air.

That night, Father Grogan came round to see them, to see that they had enough to eat. He had a letter with him too, a grubby letter, opened and closed by parish priests all over Boston, a letter that had been sent from Ireland nearly nine months before and simply addressed to 'The Kennedy Family, Boston.' Eamonn was the last Kennedy on Father Grogan's list. He knew at once the letter was for him.

He had never seen any other handwriting like Kate's loopy scrawl. Eamonn had heard Kate's mother saying she took more time over the loops on her y's and g's than she did for a whole wordful of other letters. The postmark on the grubby letter Father Grogan held out to Eamonn was almost all rubbed out and illegible. It was impossible to tell which town it had come from, but there was no mistaking the writer.

ELEVEN

Kate's letter spoke just like Kate. She started off by shouting at him.

'Why have we heard nothing from you? I thought you would send us word when you got to Liverpool. Now, for all we know, you could have drowned off the coast of Ireland. They say there was a terrible storm that night when you went aboard and set sail for England. Why didn't you write to us?'

It had been easier to forget Kate, the money she had given him and the help Eamonn's family had received from her stepmother and her grandfather. It had been easier for Eamonn to push all that to the back of his mind than to think about her and how disappointed she would be with his life in America. He wanted to write to her, but not yet, not until he had started earning good enough money to pay her back and to get all his family back together.

Kate wrote hardly anything about Ireland, but enough to tell him her stepmother and grandfather were still working hard with their soup kitchens, arguing with the British government officials and trying to get more money for the poor people. 'There's less call for the fever tents now,' Kate wrote. 'There was less fever when it got cold.'

She finished her letter with her father's address in Boston.

'He wrote to my stepmother after you set sail for America. That was when he knew I was staying here in Ireland with her. He said we were to tell you he will help you if you go to see him at his works.'

Eamonn folded the letter up and crammed it quickly back in its envelope. He was angry. How could Kate believe they would be that desperate? Her father had walked out one day and left his second wife and their children and Kate, just walked out and abandoned them and not even told them where he was going.

It was only after his wife had given him up for dead and gone to live with Kate's grandfather that letters from him, addressed only to Kate, started arriving. And the whole time he had been living a cosy life, safe from the hunger and fever in Ireland. He must have known that his wife and children were in danger while he was living a good life in Boston. Back home in Ireland Eamonn had hated the man, without ever meeting him, for leaving Kate and her family behind. How could Kate believe they would be desperate enough to take help from a man like that?

'It's none of my business,' said Mr Brady, 'but is it good news or bad?'

'Read me your letter, Eamonn.' Annie climbed onto his knee. 'I never got a letter in my whole life. What does it say?' She pulled at the corner of the envelope and a ripped piece of paper came away in her hand.

Eamonn smiled. 'It's from a girl I knew in Ireland. It says she knows a man who will give us money whenever we need it.'

Annie jumped off his knee and clapped and took a running jump at Mr Brady. With her arms hanging round his neck, her face shining with excitement, she said, 'We need money now. Shall I come and get some money with you, Eamonn? I can help you to carry it.'

Eamonn let the grubby envelope fall on the floor. 'We don't need money that badly,' he said. 'We'll never need money that badly.'

Annie pestered him. She hopped down out of Mr Brady's arms and picked the envelope up again. 'You don't need the money, Eamonn. But Mrs Brady needs the money.'

'We have to pay the rent next week, and I don't know where the money's coming from.'

Mrs Brady looked over at her husband, but he nodded at Eamonn. 'The union'll help us find the rent for another week or two. Or we can try the parish. Eamonn's right not to take money if he feels it's badly come by.'

Eamonn opened up the letter again. 'All I know about this man is that he walked out and left his family without saying goodbye, without even a word to any of them. They thought he was dead. And all the time he was having a good life here in Boston.'

'What sort of a man is that, as could walk out and leave his little children?' Mrs Brady sat down and was immediately covered with little ones, one on each knee.

'I never met him,' Eamonn said. 'Only his wife and his sons and daughter. They didn't sit around feeling sorry for themselves as long as I knew them. They were helping everyone else in Tullamore. So I never heard much about him.' Then Eamonn pointed to the address Kate had given him for her father.

'Looks like a mill-owner.'

Annie swung her arms around Mr Brady's neck again from behind and made him carry her on his back. 'Well, he won't give us no money, will he?'

And Mr Brady smiled and carried her round the room. 'Annie's right. A mill-owner wouldn't give us any help, anyway. He's bound to have heard about our strike at Kerry Mills. We're going to have to look somewhere else for work.'

Eamonn had had months of finding out what it was like to look for work if you were Irish, when he had first arrived in Boston. They had been stupid to go on strike and risk losing their jobs. But he set out every morning, as they all did, and every night they came home without work.

Sometimes Eamonn tried to take on a Boston accent, but nobody was fooled. Even when he knocked on a door where the card advertising HELP WANTED didn't say, 'No Irish Need Apply', people seemed to know he was Irish as soon as they opened the door. Sometimes they were polite and said they already had all the help they needed and they'd just forgotten to take the card out of the window. And sometimes they were rough.

At one big house, the manservant who opened the door said, 'I don't think she'll take you, but the mistress wants to see everyone who comes herself. She likes to speak to them, especially if they're Irish.'

Eamonn had to wait in the boot and shoe room behind the kitchen, where the smell of hot stew cooking made his belly ache. He was never actually hungry any more, but he never really had enough to eat.

On one wall of the room, shelves of boots and shoes reached from the floor to the ceiling, with a wooden step that you could move around to reach the top shelves. On the end wall, under a tall window with twenty panes of shining glass, there was a mahogany chest with deep, shallow drawers. One of the drawers had been pulled out and left open just before Eamonn arrived and was filled with a single layer of thick woollen knee socks, pairs of socks neatly bundled, in every colour you could imagine.

Everything was quiet, apart from the noise of the cook whisking eggs with a beater against her copper bowl. And someone was chopping on a board, onions or parsley, and singing at the same time. Eamonn pulled out another drawer in the mahogany chest. That was filled with neatly laid out pairs of finer socks in different colours. The next drawer was full of the finest socks in black and navy, silk they must have been. Eamonn closed the drawers.

There were names on the shelves of shoes, name cards in brass plates, and one person's name was attached to one whole shelf. Even the tiny shoes. There was one shelf labelled 'Miss Grace', with boots and shoes enough to fill a shop. They looked the right size to fit Annie. Annie went barefoot most of the time, though Mrs Brady had managed to get her a pair of boy's boots two sizes too big to keep her warm in the winter. Eamonn looked at the shelf of shoes that were just in Annie's size, where there were three pairs of red boots, almost identical. He listened again in case someone was coming to get him and then reached out and touched the pair nearest to him. The leather was as soft as a woollen blanket. He lifted up the small boot and the leather sole was completely clean and unscratched as if the boots had never been worn. The next pair of red boots had the tiniest scratches on the soles, as if they had been worn once.

Eamonn put the boots down carefully and stepped back, holding his hands behind his back. His fingers burned. There was so much there, in that one room. The room where they kept their boots and shoes was larger and brighter than the cellar kitchen where the Brady family lived and cooked and ate their meals together. And there were so many boots and shoes and socks. Had they counted them? Did the family who lived in this house even know how many they had? Would they notice if Eamonn took a pair of soft, red boots to give to Annie, the oldest pair that had been worn a bit? Would anybody even notice?

The door opened. The manservant who came in looked straight towards the open sock drawer and scanned it, as if he were counting the socks. There were so many socks there. Why did it matter if any of them were missing? Were they testing him to see if he was honest? Perhaps that was a good sign. Perhaps that meant they would give him a job, since he hadn't stolen anything.

'My mistress wants you to come upstairs.'

From the green, sparkling stone floor of the basement, Eamonn climbed stairs and stepped onto a carpet whose softness almost knocked him off balance, as if he were walking on a deep sprung mattress. From upstairs, much higher on a landing two floors up, Eamonn heard the sound of children laughing and then fighting and then laughing and chasing each other again. Then he was shown into the drawing room.

A woman in black sat near the window on a green velvet sofa, with two younger women in green flowered chairs nearby. She pointed to a flower in the carpet. 'Have you wiped your feet, boy?'

Eamonn nodded.

'Then stand there.'

The three women looked at Eamonn and then at each other, looked at him and then back again at each other.

'You are Irish, are you not?' The woman had an accent that sounded quite different to the Americans he heard out on the streets of Boston. Eamonn nodded. 'Yes, madam.'

'I don't like the Irish.'

Eamonn looked beyond the three women, out of the window. Across the street there were other grand houses. Did the same people live in all of them?

'Catholic too, I don't doubt?'

'Yes, madam.'

'The Catholics are lazy and don't provide for their families properly. They expect us to look after their children, however many they bring into the world.' She was talking now more to her young friends than to Eamonn. Then she looked straight at Eamonn again. 'I don't like immigrants. And I most particularly do not like Irish Catholic immigrants. What are you doing here?'

'I saw the card in your window, madam, which said you needed a helper.'

'But what on earth are you doing in Boston? Why are you not back in Ireland where you belong?'

Eamonn started to explain, quietly, but she shouted at him and told him to speak up. 'We needed work, madam. And we didn't have enough to eat.'

'So you thought you would come here and take the bread out of the mouths of the deserving poor in America, did you? Mmm?' She turned to the young women who were sitting with her, taking turns to stare at Eamonn and then look at their hostess before they drank more tea. 'They don't have to come here, you know.' The older woman carried on as if Eamonn had already left the room. 'They say they're destitute. They say they've no money and no food, but if you ask me, they bring it on themselves.' Then she turned and spoke directly to Eamonn again. 'Nobody asked you Irish to come here, young man.' She took a sip of her tea. 'I mean you no harm, but you really would have a better life if you all went back home, back where you belong in Ireland.' Then she nodded to the manservant and turned away.

The words scratched at Eamonn's eyes and made them sting. 'They bring it on themselves.' From the upstairs floors, a piano was being played and children, younger children like Annie and Shaun, were playing some sort of a party game. 'They bring it on themselves. They don't have to come here, you know.'

Eamonn was glad he hadn't reached out and pocketed a pair of the beautiful socks, a pair of the soft, red leather boots for Annie to look smart in when they went to church. He was glad he was leaving that house and taking nothing with him. But the words would never leave him. He wanted to reach to the top shelf in the boot room and run his hands along the shelves and knock the rows of shoes onto the floor, all the boots and shoes. He wished he could have taken the drawers and drawers of socks and shaken them out and thrown them into the gutter.

But he left the neat rows of shoes and boots, the carefully arranged drawers full of socks, the beautifully written labels on the shelves, the flowered carpets, and the velvet sofas. He left all of that behind and took only the hard, ugly words. 'They bring it on themselves. They don't have to come here, you know.'

Annie couldn't find a job either, since all she could do was mill work. They didn't want her walking too far, and the mills close by wouldn't have her. And then one day in the park Annie got what Joe called the chance of a lifetime. A very wealthy couple, a surgeon and his wife, saw her out with all the others and decided they wanted to adopt her.

Eamonn and Joe had taken the little ones out again, walking all the way to the park on the other side of Boston where Eamonn had stayed in his first two months. And while they were swinging from one of the trees with its great, strong branches the lady and gentleman walking by had asked them about Annie. She looked quite different to all the rest of the children, with her white-blonde curls grown back again, though not as long as they were before the accident. The others had black or dark brown hair. It was obvious that Annie wasn't their sister.

Then Dr and Mrs Poole talked to Annie.

'Where's your mother, dear? Is she here in Boston?'

'I don't know.'

'And your father? Is he back in Ireland?'

'How should I know?' Annie ran away from them and threw herself at the tree branch, swinging herself now and not waiting for Joe or Eamonn to help. The doctor and his wife told Eamonn they would be happy to adopt her and take her to live with them in their large house close by, on the good side of Boston. They had no children of their own, they said. And besides, they felt everyone should do their bit for the Irish poor.

They handed Eamonn a visiting card, and the lady held Annie's grubby hand and told her about the lovely room she would have and the toys and dresses they could buy together.

But Annie wasn't interested. 'I'm staying with you,' she said, pulling Eamonn's hair and running away to make him chase her.

Mr Brady was furious when he heard about the offer. 'They can't just buy our children like you'd buy a pet dog. Annie can't go off with anyone—just because they've got money and we've got none. She's part of our family now.' Annie launched herself onto his back again and then climbed over his shoulder and sat in his lap.

'I'm not going nowhere without all yous.'

The union got them the money to pay their rent. That was after Mr Brady had gone to the charities to ask for money, and no one would help him. They said he had only himself to blame for not having any money. They called it 'voluntary destitution' because he had gone on strike and said the only money they could give him was the money to buy a ticket back to Ireland. So all the time they looked for work, Mrs Brady's money paid for their food and the men and women from the union collected for them to help them pay their rent.

Eamonn gave all his money to help the Bradys. He had nothing left to save for the rest of his family, if ever he found out where they were. He had heard nothing from his mother. He held on to the hope that the doctor would have written to him—probably before he left the Buchanans' farm—if his mother had died of the fever. So somewhere she must be alive. And he assumed that Dermot and Shaun were safe.

Sometimes he thought that Shaun must have forgotten him, in the same way that Annie had forgotten everything about her life before the Kerry Mills. But he kept quiet. He couldn't talk about his family to the Bradys as long as they all had no work and no idea how long the unions could help them.

In the end there was only one thing left to try. Eamonn had tramped the whole city in search of any place that would take a young Irish boy who had hardly been to school and had never learned a trade. Mr Brady and Joe had gone even further afield, walking out to the farms outside Boston where people said there was always work to be had. But the work had always gone by the time they'd arrived.

They had even talked for days about going west, joining the train of people travelling west towards California in search of a new life over there. Joe took Annie along to a public meeting where they talked of the fortunes people had made, picking up buckets of gold with their bare hands out of the river. And they said there was enough for everyone. There was no limit to the fortunes people could make from the gold there was just lying around, waiting to be picked up off the ground in California.

Mrs Brady was worried about the Indians, but Joe had an answer to that. 'They're all friendly Indians out there. They told us at the meeting. There's friendly Indians and there's Indians that shoot at people. And the ones in California are friendly ones. They don't mind people coming and taking their gold. There's enough for everyone.'

Mr Brady had other worries. 'What sort of people are they if all they care about is just walking round picking up buckets of gold? I'm not sure I want the children growing up with them sort of characters.'

'I never knew you would object to walking around picking up a bucket of gold. What's wrong with a bucket of gold every now and then?' Mrs Brady gave him a dig in the ribs but her husband had his ideas fixed.

'There's more important things.'

'Not when you haven't got any money at all.'

The argument didn't go on for long. They couldn't go to California anyway. If you wanted to go in a wagon to California, you had to have your own wagon and food and even guns, and then you had to pay some money to go with the whole train of wagons and a guide. It was only the ones who had money who could make money. They would have to keep on searching for real work.

Eamonn knew he owed it to the Bradys to try to get work with Kate's father. It was the last thing he had ever wanted to do. He was angry at Kate for believing they could be desperate enough to ask her father for help. And he was angry because they *were* so desperate. He owed it to the Brady family and to Annie to try and get work wherever he could.

Galway Mills wasn't a cotton mill. It was a garment factory where they made fine men's shirts and working overalls. It was closer to their street than Eamonn had realized, no more than a good half hour's walk through narrow cobbled streets and then across the river. Eamonn told no one where he was going. He had gone halfway there several times before. Whenever he had been to get another job and been turned down and cursed at for being Irish he had tried to make up for the insults by starting to walk to the place where he knew they would almost certainly get work if he mentioned Kate's name.

Kate's father had a nerve. How could he leave Kate and her stepmother alone in Ireland and then pretend he was good and generous offering work to the Irish in Boston. What good was it to be generous to strangers if you kicked your own family and left them to take care of themselves? Eamonn had left his own family hundreds of miles behind him. He had left Shaun with strangers and now he was looking after Annie. But that was different. He hadn't been able to help doing what he did. There was nothing he could have done for his family if he had stayed behind in Canada. He had had to leave.

He stood at the factory gates. He could not bring himself to speak to Kate's father. But there was a notice which said, HELP WANTED. APPLY WITHIN. Maybe he wouldn't have to see the owner. Maybe he could just slip in and work there without ever having to speak to Mr Burke.

The man in the gatehouse had a Galway accent.

'And where are you from?'

Eamonn never knew what to answer to a question like that. Did the man mean, what part of Boston did he live in, or was he from Ireland? And did he want to know how Eamonn had got to Boston? Did he want to know about Grosse Isle and the long journey they had come?

'I'm from Ireland.'

Eamonn twisted at the button on his braces, right where Mrs Brady had told him not to twist at the button or he would have to sew it on himself next time.

'I can tell you're from Ireland.' The gatehouse man sat down with a pencil and a large book. 'Whereabouts in Ireland are you from?'

'I was born in Ballinglas, sir.' Eamonn tried to see what was already written in the book. 'But we had to leave our village when they cleared it, sir. And then we went to Tullamore.'

'And would you know the Aylmers in Tullamore? And the baker? What was his name?'

Eamonn knew all the people the man at the gate was talking about. Waves of relief swept over him at finding, in a Boston factory, a man who spoke his own language, a man who must understand what they had been through. And he sat down and told the gatehouse man, Flanagan he was called, everything that had happened from them leaving Ballinglas to his time in Boston.

'There's work enough for all of you here,' Flanagan said. He picked a large black book off one of the shelves which ran across the window behind him. Through the window, Eamonn could see men in blue overalls moving quickly across the courtyard with bundles of parcels. Flanagan glanced back at the busy scene outside his window and then down at the book.

'We've just taken on new orders for a big store in New York and there's more coming in for the stores in Boston.'

He took a pair of spectacles out of his overall pocket, put them on and then looked over the top of them at

Eamonn before he looked in his big black book again. 'We need people who can use sewing machines. We need cutters. We need cleaners. And we need two good messenger lads.'

Then Flanagan put down his glasses on the counter between them.

'Mind, the boss won't have any young ones here.' He flicked through the pages of his book again and pointed to his lists of names at the front of the book, with the date of birth in a column on the right.

'Not as young as seven years old. She should be put to school, if you've a seven year old. And if that's hard, you can ask the master and he might just help yous with the school money. But he won't have young ones working when they should be put to school.'

Eamonn had no idea what Annie would say about the idea of joining the others at school. The little Brady children had all been at school since they were five and Annie, at seven, could neither read nor write. She probably couldn't sit still for very long either. Eamonn remembered the hours they had had to sit and learn tables or listen to the teacher reading aloud to them as they sat on hard benches in the little school in Ballinglas. But it was good to be able to read and write.

When Flanagan had heard Eamonn read and given him some writing to do, he said he would be sending Eamonn up to be a messenger boy for the factory. 'And after that you can be one of the clerks,' he said, 'and maybe one day your own boss. Anyone can read and write like you do will go far.'

Mr Brady came up to the factory the day after. He saw Flanagan and the foreman at the factory and talked about all the jobs he had had before. Then Eamonn gasped, standing with his hands clasped tightly behind his back to stop himself pulling at his braces and twisting at the buttons that were always falling off.

'I have to tell you, sir, I am a union man.'

Mr Brady stood respectfully enough, while Flanagan and the foreman sat and looked at him. He didn't look like a troublemaker. Why did he have to tell them all that right now, before he had even got the job? The family desperately needed money. Why didn't Mr Brady keep quiet about the union? Joe Brady was the same.

'I'm in the union, sir,' he said. He was already taller than his father and stood proudly in front of the two men who gave out all the jobs at Galway Mills.

'And why is that?' The foreman looked at Flanagan. 'You won't need your unions here. Our boss is the best there is in the whole of this state. You won't find a better. He treats his workers properly and he expects good work from you.' He glanced sideways at Flanagan again and then asked both men, 'Are you telling me you're troublemakers?'

Joe looked at his father, waiting for him to say the first word, but when it didn't come he answered for both of them. 'The union has been good to us, sir. We owe it to our people in the union to work with them and collect money for them if they need help.'

Then Flanagan, who had been all friendliness to Eamonn the day before, turned to him. 'And what about you, laddie? You never told me any of this. Does this mean you're in the union too?'

Eamonn looked at Mr Brady, but there was no help coming from him. Why did they have to mention it in the first place? The family needed money. It was the union who had been giving them money, but that couldn't go on forever.

'Yes, I'm in the union, sir. They have been good to all of us. We can't leave the union, sir.'

The silence in the room dragged Eamonn's hopes down, like the strong current just before a canoe reaches wild, white water.

A delivery arrived, pulled by two heavy horses, and the foreman went out into the yard and showed the driver where to take his load. And still Flanagan said nothing. Then the foreman came back.

'All right?' He nodded at Flanagan. 'Has he told you when you can turn in for work?' Then he smiled. 'I'm off back to the job. It's a seven o'clock start, mind. Union or no union.' And he winked at Eamonn and walked out. Then Flanagan wrote their names in his book while he told them about the boss.

'He doesn't mind the union.' He took a long ruler and drew a line under their names. 'As long as they do what he says. The only thing he won't have is when anyone tries to keep someone out if there's work to be done. The man as did this job before me, he was only giving work to Galway men. Turning the others away, he was, even the Americans who've lived here a good few years. He was turning them all away and keeping the work for his cousins. The boss wouldn't have that. He says there has to be work for anyone who'll work hard, as long as we've work to give.'

Mrs Brady got a job there next, a few weeks after they all started. They said you had to have experience using a sewing machine, and there was good money to be made if you could use one. Better than cleaning floors at the other end of the city, at any rate. So she stayed behind at her cleaning job and got the housekeeper to show her how to use the sewing machine there, and never stopped talking about the wonderful sewing you could do with a machine until Mr Brady shut her up with, 'When I'm a millionaire, I'll buy you a sewing machine, first thing, and you can sit and sew all day.'

The machines in the factory were even better than the one she had used at her old cleaning job—the very latest thing—and she insisted she never got tired of sewing.

Eamonn could see why she liked her work. He went in and out of the factory every day, running with messages backwards and forwards between the offices and the shop floor. He saw rows and rows of women buzzing away at their shiny machines and somehow managing to talk above the noise. Mrs Brady said it made a change to be in a place where she had people to talk to. In her cleaning job, she had been told to keep quiet and get on with her work, and even the cook and the housekeeper had considered themselves above her. She said she thought the only reason they had shown her how to use the sewing machine was because they thought she would do some of their sewing work for free.

Annie didn't like school.

In the mill, she had been everybody's special pet. They loved her white blonde curly hair and the quick, jolly way she went about her work, running to fetch something for them whenever they had dropped it, darting in and out among the looms, tying up broken threads. Everyone said they didn't know what they would do without her, even the foreman who had let her go when the strike spoiled everything.

But at school they treated her as if she was stupid. She was seven and couldn't read, so they put her with the five year olds. Soon most of them had learned to read. Annie was still not very tall, but everyone knew she was seven. She was desperate to learn to read, to catch up with the others and get in the group with her own age. Some of the seven year olds were already monitors, sitting and teaching the smaller ones their alphabet. Annie had never felt stupid in her life before.

There was another thing. The teachers shouted at her and said she didn't listen properly, so she got caned and made to stand at the back of the class. But it wasn't that she didn't listen. She didn't hear. She wasn't deaf. She heard when people looked at her and talked in the room at home, but in a classroom, with groups of children reading out loud to their monitors and with others saying their tables, she only picked up some of the sounds. A lot of the words just didn't make sense. She saw teachers shouting at her from the front of the room. She knew they were shouting at her, but the words they were saying got lost and the next thing she knew they were marching her out to the back of the class. She longed to go back to the factory, where she could get on with the job she was good at.

Annie pleaded with Eamonn to help her. 'Teach me to read, Eamonn. You've got to teach me to read so those old crabs leave me alone.' And Eamonn read to her and she read back because she remembered, but she couldn't read the same words again on a different page.

'Ah, will you leave the child alone and stop tormenting her?' Mr Brady liked to read. He had a small stock of books from Ireland and kept talking about joining up to the circulating library when they had a bit of money left over. He used to sit Annie on his knee and any other child who was around and read to them without making them read to him. 'There's people that can read and people that never learns to read, if you ask me. They're just made like that. Just look at Mrs Brady there.' His wife was stitching at an embroidered table cloth, a cloth that looked far too grand for the scratched old table someone had left behind in their cellar kitchen. 'Mrs Brady can't read for the life of her.'

She smiled and nodded. Eamonn had heard her story often before. She had been to school and then been taken out of school because her father died. Then she had been to school again for a year when she was eight, and then been put into service. No one knew why she never learned to read.

'But it's not for want of brains,' Mr Brady always said. 'She's the cleverest woman I know.' And he would point to the embroidery she was doing, or the meal she was cooking, or the things she taught her children. 'You can't do that kind of work without you've got brains.' He puzzled about it every time they talked about Annie and the reading and how she hated school. 'There must be different kinds of brains. That's all I can say. There must be them as are good with books and them as are good with making things.'

'And them like you,' Mrs Brady would say, 'as can talk the back legs off a donkey.'

TWELVE

A month after they started work at Galway Mills, Eamonn had still not met Kate's father, the man who owned the factory. He had no idea what he looked like. And none of the Bradys knew that the factory where Eamonn had finally found them all work was the same one mentioned in the letter from Kate. There was no need to tell them.

After a month, Eamonn was able to start again, trying to save money to get his family back together. He hadn't mentioned his family for a long time. But Mr Brady wouldn't let him forget them. So Eamonn wrote letters again—to the priest at the church he had gone to with the Buchanans, to Grosse Isle where the doctor might still have news of his mother. While he was waiting for an answer to his letters, all he could do was to save his money, knowing the saving could take years.

They gave Eamonn a smart uniform to wear after his first month was over, because they said he would have to take messages from the owner to the bank or to another office. Eamonn dreaded having to meet Kate's father. Ever since he had got to know Kate, in Tullamore, he had been angry with the man who had left Kate and her stepmother behind. He just didn't recognize this man in the picture everyone else painted of a factory owner who sounded more like a saint.

He was different to the other factory owners because he wouldn't take on children as workers. Some people said that showed how good he was. Other people said he was taking bread out of the mouths of families who needed their children to work and he shouldn't be the one to decide what people ought to do with their children.

He was different because he wouldn't let his foreman keep out workers from another part of the country. Most of the owners couldn't care less what their foremen did, as long as the work got done. He was different because they got their money every Friday and there was never any docked except for lateness. When word got round the union, everybody wanted to work at Galway Mills. Everybody said, like Flanagan the gatehouse man, that he was the best factory owner in the whole of Boston.

Only Eamonn knew he had walked out and left his family. But hadn't he made up for leaving his family by looking after two hundred other families through his factory? Eamonn was glad he didn't have to meet him.

Mr Burke, the owner, had a secretary who came downstairs and clapped his hands when there was something to be done. They said he had a suite of rooms, a drawing room and grand offices, up the stairs beyond the main office where Eamonn worked until he was needed to run errands. But Eamonn never went there and he never saw his employer arriving or going home.

Then one day the secretary tapped his way downstairs and clapped his hands. 'You're wanted, boy.' The secretary had brilliant white cuffs peeping out below his jacket sleeves and he tugged at them if ever they dared to creep out of sight. 'Mr Burke wants to give you a message personally. Let me look at you.' He took a handkerchief and swiped it over the dark fronts of Eamonn's waistcoat. Then he gave his red bow tie a tweak. 'You'll do. Up there. He's waiting for you.' And the secretary turned his back on Eamonn and strolled off importantly, hands behind his back, on one of his promenades around the factory floor.

The door at the top of the stairs was open. Through a small entrance lobby, Eamonn saw a blue sofa, and then another. A huge window threw light on pale blue walls, card tables, a china cabinet, and a scattering of comfortable chairs on the grey patterned carpet. The room was empty and the door at the far end was open. Eamonn hesitated and called out and then, when there was no answer, walked across the drawing room and tapped at the open door. A voice told him to enter.

There was another huge window, like the one in the drawing room, and in front of the window, which looked out over the factory yard, there was a large mahogany desk. The man at the desk raised his head but didn't look round.

'Thank you for coming. It's an urgent message. I've nearly finished. Wait there a second, will you?' And he waved his right hand to the right of his desk so that Eamonn was standing just behind him as he wrote. There were pictures on the desk, in silver frames. One was a small painting of a factory with round towers, like the places where they make whiskey, and one was a painting of a dog. But at the very front of the group of pictures was a studio photograph of a woman who looked like Kate, with a baby girl dressed in white lace, sitting on her knee. There was a palm tree behind them.

The pen scratched gently at the paper. Eamonn frowned. He couldn't stop himself. He stared at the picture and all his anger at Kate's father came back to him. What had he done to make her die, that beautiful woman who must be Kate's mother? And why had he walked out and left Kate and her stepmother and her brothers? And how could he sit there, in his wealthy office in Boston, with secretaries and messenger boys and money papering the walls around him when his wife was nursing people dying of the fever?

'I won't be a second. It's good of you to take this for me.'

Kate's father kept on writing. He looked up for a second and stared at the photograph then carried on writing. Finally he signed his name with a flourish, blotted the paper, folded it and handed it to Eamonn. Then he looked closely at him. After a while he smiled. 'I told them to send me the fastest, most reliable messenger. So that's you, is it? What's your name?'

Eamonn's first name said nothing about him. 'Eamonn, sir. Shall I be off now, sir?'

Kate's father was younger than he had expected. He was a handsome man, when Eamonn had been picturing someone whose whole face marked him out as evil. It was easy to understand why the people in his factory said he was the best of men. He looked generous. He made sure his workers had everything they needed. But he had left his wife and children behind.

'And where are you from, young man?'

'From Ireland, sir.' Eamonn backed away towards the door. 'Where is the letter to go to, sir?'

Kate's father laughed. 'You're right. I haven't put a name or a street or anything at all on in my haste. If you give it back to me, I'll do that for you.'

Eamonn was forced to stand and wait again, when all he wanted to do was to get away. The letter was to go to a bank.

'They'll be giving you a reply.' Kate's father sat back in his chair and stared at the pictures on his desk, before he swivelled his chair round and looked at Eamonn. 'Come straight back to me. They'll let you up here as soon as you arrive.'

Mr Burke's bank was in the nicest part of Boston, not far from the river and the university. And no one thought to turn Eamonn away from the tall gold and black doors and the marble entrance hall in the smart uniform he was wearing. As soon as the man at the entrance saw where Eamonn came from, he was led straight through to the main banking hall to a man in frock coat and pin-striped trousers. A young man came to Eamonn with a glass of water, while the banking clerk pulled out a large book and went through rows of figures and then pulled out two other books, marked 'England' and 'Ireland'.

The clerk gave him two sealed envelopes.

'These are the drafts he needs.' He held up the second envelope and winked. 'And these are the tickets for the Irish relatives. He'll be pleased about them.'

Soon the business was done and Eamonn walked in a daze along the marble corridors out of the palace of a bank into the sunshine outside. What sort of mortals were they, who could work in a place like that? He wondered if you had to have a lot of money before you got a job there, or if it just depended on the people you knew. People who worked in a palace like the bank he had just been in and the other banks he had to walk past on his way back to the factory must earn trunkloads of money. Their clothes must cost a lot, for a start.

He had to pass by one of the newly opened department stores, with enormous shining glass windows and beautiful displays of furniture and fashions everywhere you looked. The messenger boy before him had been given a job in the factory because he dawdled too much and had ended up losing an important letter—but Eamonn could understand how that happened. It was easy to slow down and take your time on the way back to the factory with so many wonderful things to see, so many wealthy people and carriages. He wished he could show his mother the streets of Boston and the brightly coloured window displays.

The minute he thought of his mother, he started to walk more quickly again. He couldn't run all the way back to the factory. It was just too far. But the last time he had seen his mother, she had been lying on a thin mattress in a bleak hospital ward. They had been lucky to eat a bowl of porridge every day, and the only colour in their life had been the white of the hospital sheets and the glistening green of the cold stone floor.

He couldn't let himself stroll around and look at all that money, all that food displayed in the windows, when his mother was still somewhere alone up north. He had no way of explaining why he hadn't heard from his mother and brothers, in spite of the letters he had sent through the priests. Perhaps they were happy without him. Perhaps they had decided that he would be better off without them. But he knew he couldn't rest until he had got them all together.

Before he had started working for Kate's father, when they had all been out of work and desperate to find any small job that would help them to pay the rent, Eamonn hadn't been able to think beyond getting a job. Any job. Now he knew he couldn't just stay as a messenger boy. He had to become something much better, get a job where he earned the kind of money that would really help his family—not just the sort of money where he was happy to have enough to eat. He would have been happy enough with that when they were living on Grosse Isle. But now he needed the kind of money where he could do things you didn't need to do to live. He needed money to travel all the way up north, back where he had come from, money to send people out looking for his family, money to pay for their train fares and a place for them all to live in Boston. He had seen close up how some of the people lived in Boston.

Why was it some people had the money to keep more shoes and socks than anyone could ever use in their lifetime while others walked around with no shoes? Why did some women sit around their whole lives in drawing rooms, talking and doing embroidery, when his mother and Mrs Brady and even little Annie had to be up and about from early to late working, always working, and not even learning to read?

He walked faster and faster. The more he thought about the differences between the people living less than half an hour apart in Boston, the faster he walked, the letter he was carrying almost forgotten, sealed in a parcel with the gracious livery of the bank stamped all over the outside.

Kate's father was in the drawing room when he arrived

back, and the curtains were drawn. 'Can you stand at the window, young man, and open the reply letter for me? I've given myself a mighty headache and cannot read just now.'

Eamonn opened the parcel and stood with it opened, looking over to where Mr Burke was sitting in a winged chair, hunched up with his head down over his knees. He lifted his head up slightly. 'You can read, can't you?'

'Yes, sir. Shall I read it to you, sir?'

'If you'd be so kind . . .'

The letter said that tickets would be arranged for Kate, her stepmother, and the boys to travel to Boston first class by steamship and that money would be sent to them, as Mr Burke had instructed. There was a ticket too for Kate's grandfather if he wished to travel, but if he did not wish to move to America, he was to receive money from the bank every month.

'Is that all, sir? Do you need me for any other messages? They always want me downstairs, sir.' Eamonn wanted to get away, out of that room, since he was sure it must be the room that made you have a headache and feel bad. This was all too much and far too soon. There had been times when he had been afraid to admit, even to himself, that he missed Kate, that he ever wanted to see her again.

And it felt wrong to want to see her, to be turning cartwheels in his head about her coming, when his mother might still be cold or hungry somewhere up in Canada. There was another thing. Kate's coming was happening far too soon. He had only wanted to see her again when he was rich and could show off how well he'd done in America. And if Kate and her family came, who would be left in Ireland, when Eamonn wanted so badly to keep a part of Ireland in himself?

Mr Burke still sat there and said nothing. He didn't look pleased. Not like the bank man had said he would be. Eamonn folded up the letter and put it on the table nearest to him. There were footsteps, running up the stairs, a sharp knock, and the secretary walked straight in and straight over to his employer.

'You'll need to see the foreman, Mr Burke.'

He put his hand on Mr Burke's shoulder. 'There's been a strike again at Kerry Mills and there's talk of strikes all over. Will you see the foreman and the union, sir?'

Kate's father sat up very straight. He looked pale and tired. 'Send them in.' Then he pointed to Eamonn. 'And you had better stay. There may be important messages to take.'

Mr Brady came in with the foreman and both men took off their caps as Mr Burke stood up to meet them.

'What's the trouble?'

Mr Brady was fearless. He had never met his boss before, but he wasn't afraid of anyone.

'There's been a child killed, sir, down at Kerry Mills. They've done nothing about those carding machines, sir, and a child's been killed.'

'That's disgraceful news.' Mr Burke sat down again and motioned to them both to take a seat. 'Are you getting a fund up for their families? You can put me down to give some money. And see what else we can do for them.'

'We have to go on strike, sir.'

'But why, man? Striking won't bring the child back.'

'Nor won't money either, sir, if you don't mind my saying so.'

'But why strike here? You know my views. I won't have children working. I won't put children's lives and health at risk.'

'Then make the others see it your way, sir. Make the other owners pay a better wage so people don't have to put their children out to work.'

'I can't make them do anything. Every mill-owner does as he wants to. They won't listen to me.'

'But they'll have to listen to us, sir. If every worker goes on strike. If none of the mills can work. You owners'll have to get together and find a way to make your places safe for children.'

'But why are you aiming your strike against me? You know I support you.'

'It's not against you, sir. We've all got nothing against you. But the only way we'll win is to stand together.'

'You know you won't be paid, don't you?'

Mr Brady nodded.

'How will you manage without pay?'

'With the union we'll manage, sir.'

Then Mr Burke turned to Eamonn. 'I'll need you to wait now, young man. I'll have to send messages.'

Eamonn moved forward and then looked at Mr Brady, wanting to be told what to do. But Mr Brady just nodded. 'It's up to you, youngster,' he said. 'You do what you think's right.'

Eamonn walked towards Mr Brady and the door. Then he turned round. 'I'm sorry, sir,' he said. 'I'm in the union too. We've got to do something for the children at Kerry Mills. My friend, our little sister, Annie, nearly got herself killed there.'

Kate's father slumped back into his chair. It was impossible to tell whether he was angry about the strike or about the child who had died. Eamonn had no idea what would happen next. He had no idea whether they would all lose their jobs or how long the strike would last. All he knew was that his savings would get eaten up again and that the moment when he could go and fetch his family was fading further and further away into the distance.

But now he saw, much more clearly, why they had to go on strike. He'd seen enough, in Ireland, where Kate's family had kept his own family alive. He'd seen enough, in Boston, where Kate's father, who wasn't a saint whatever people said, was still the only mill-owner who kept children away from machines. He'd seen enough to know that when evil things happened in the world, when children died of hunger or got dragged inside machines, it wasn't because the world was filled with evil people. It was because the good people were too scared to rise up and do something. Someone had to do something; they had to go on strike.

By the time they got outside to the factory gate, a procession had already gathered, a long line of men and women from other mills, carrying banners. Annie was there, instead of being at school, and was holding one of the strings of their banner as the workers from Galway Mills joined the procession and headed down towards Kerry Mills.

Eamonn walked on in silence, in among the crowd, with the Brady family at its head. He was torn apart with guilt. Whatever he did was wrong. He was torn apart because he had no idea any longer what he wanted. Whatever he wanted was wrong. Only that morning, walking quickly through the banking quarter and then through the fashionable shopping streets, he had been making plans to make lots of money, more money than anyone could ever really use. And all the time he had been thinking of ways to make money, some child as young as Annie, as young as his brother Shaun, had been working and then struggling to stay alive after the machines had dragged them in.

But if he didn't try to make some money he would never see his mother and brothers again. And the families who had sent their children to work at Kerry Mills had only been trying to make money. It was easy for people to say money wasn't important. It was easy for them to say school was more important. Children's safety was more important. It was easy to say that for people who had enough money and had enough for their children to eat. In front of him were Mr and Mrs Brady with no money and all of their children to feed. Eamonn caught up with Mr Brady and asked him, 'What will we do for money now, eh? And what will we do if we lose?'

Mr Brady looked grim and then smiled and then frowned again and then waved at the crowd of people in their procession. 'We're not going to lose this time. Look at all these people. This is America. We shouldn't have to choose between letting our children starve to death because we have no money to buy food and letting them get killed by machines. This is America, Eamonn.'

The strike spread and the news of it spread, much more quickly than the first one. At every public meeting, Annie jumped up on a box beside Mr Brady while he spoke to the crowds about the day they had gone on strike to make sure she wasn't forced to go in underneath a working machine. And Annie pulled her hair aside to show how the blonde curls covered the scar where her hair would never grow back.

'Would you let your child be treated like that?' Mr Brady would shout. And the crowds shouted back, 'Never. Never.' And he drowned out their shouts with his own, 'Well, that's what the mill-owners want to do to all of our children.'

Mrs Brady used to stand on the edge of the crowd hearing him speak, and watching the faces light up as he set the crowds on fire with his anger.

'I think he likes the being on strike better than when he goes to work,' she whispered to Eamonn. Her pride in her husband was warmer than any expensive fur coat, brighter than any diamond ring. 'That's when he comes alive.'

With this strike his speeches started to work, to be heard beyond the streets around the mills. The politicians got involved. All over the state there was an outcry about the danger children were in when they worked. The union people stuck together. Not a single mill in Massachusetts went to work. People who had nothing to do with the unions brought them food. People who said, 'I don't hold with unions. But you're doing a grand job,' gave them money.

The strike ended, four weeks after it had started, with an agreement by all the mill-owners to make sure that none of them made children do dangerous work. The workers marched back to their factories with banners flying. And at Galway Mills they were soon all working through the night to catch up on late orders.

Then Eamonn could see how strong they were, in the union. He could forget the times when he had had to be frightened of any employer, when he knew he had to try to be invisible in case he might annoy the boss and get the sack. They had left their boss for four long weeks with no one to do the work and then they had all got back their jobs. Together they were strong. Mr Brady was right. This was America. No one could treat one of them badly without having to face up to all of them.

The next time he had to go into Mr Burke's office to take a message, he looked a little too long at the photograph in the silver frame. Mr Burke followed his gaze.

'That's my first wife,' he said. 'She died in Ireland. And that's my daughter, Kate.'

'What did she die of?'

'She died in childbirth, with my second child.'

Eamonn had already overstepped the mark, but he didn't stop.

'And are your children all dead too?'

Mr Burke shook his head. 'But they're not yet here in Boston.' He picked up the photo frame and looked at it and then turned it onto its face. 'I married again. My wife and family are still in Ireland.'

'And you left them behind,' Eamonn shouted. The sound of his own shouting shocked him, like a gun going off too close to his ear. Then he turned and walked through the door to the drawing room and right through to the lobby that led downstairs. Now he'd done it. What the strike hadn't managed to do he had done for himself. He was bound to have lost his job for speaking out to the boss like that. Even Mr Brady wouldn't have spoken like that to the boss. Mr Brady was always polite, whatever he had to say. But Eamonn had shouted at the boss and walked out on him. Now he had nothing to lose. He turned around and ran the whole length of the drawing room, across the thick carpet and into the office.

'How could you do it?' he shouted. 'You're supposed to be so good. Everyone says you're a good man. But you left your wife and family behind. They helped us in Tullamore. They're helping other people now. And all the people dying out there. They could have died. And you never even wrote to them for years. How could you do that?'

Eamonn's hands were clenched into fists, ready to punch out at anyone who challenged him. He stepped back, away from Kate's father, frightened of his own anger. But Mr Burke was calm.

'You know my daughter and my wife?' he said. Then he nodded. 'Of course you do. You're the boy my Katy is pining to hear from. Have you written to them since you arrived in North America? Have you even told them that you got here safely?'

Eamonn was silent and Kate's father continued, 'I know you haven't, because they think you haven't arrived yet. Kate has written to me about the boy who left her behind.' He smiled, and tried to get Eamonn to sit down on the chair at the other side of his huge desk, but Eamonn stood on the same spot, hands and arms rigid by his sides, like a soldier on parade.

'You've decided you're not going to write to them until you're a rich American. Isn't that right?'

Eamonn glared at Kate's father, but his anger was all washed out.

'How do I know all that?' Kate's father sat down and picked up the photograph again. 'I came here with no money. I ran away from them because the distillery was losing money and I'd have had to ask my wife for money to keep it going. And more than that. I ran away because Kate was growing up.'

Eamonn looked straight at the photo, of the woman who looked like Kate, while her father carried on.

'It was Kate I couldn't stand, the looking at her and remembering my first wife. I started to go mad, with no money left and the ghost of my first wife staring at me through Kate. You're right to be angry with me. I ran away and left my family because I was going mad. And after that, after I came here and came to my senses, I was ashamed. I thought my wife would hate me. I thought she would never have me back. So I worked away to make money to bring them all together here. And still I was too ashamed of what I'd done. It was only Katy I could write to. In the end she wrote to me and told me she didn't want to hear anything more from me if I ignored her stepmother. I had to do something about it then. I never wanted to lose my family. Now they're all coming here, to be with me.'

Eamonn sat down on the floor. He thought he had calmed down now, but still he pulled at his red bow tie so hard that the knot got tighter instead of unravelling. He bit his lips and took an age to untie the thing and lay it down beside him. He tugged at the laces on his polished, black boots and set the boots down neatly on the floor.

'I know you'll be telling me to go,' he said.

He stood up and took off the short blue jacket he'd been given for visits to banks. He felt stupid and awkward and useless. He felt as if he had been tricked into making the kind of a bargain he would never have chosen to make. He felt as if he should have known all along that some evil spirit was forcing him to give away his mother's life and his brothers' safety in exchange for the happiness of seeing Kate again. And what sort of happiness could that bring him now?

He didn't want to see Kate again. He didn't want Kate to see him. He didn't want Kate to know he had failed in everything he had set out to do. He had failed to look after his family. He had failed to become a rich American. He had failed to earn so much money that he could pay her back ten times what he owed her. He had failed.

Of course he wanted to see her. Yes. But no, he didn't want to see her. Not if seeing Kate meant he would never see his mother and brothers again. No. Kate had seen enough in Ireland, enough of him failing and letting his family down. He didn't want her to see him. And now he had thrown away his job, he had made quite sure he wouldn't be seeing her.

'I'm not telling you to go, laddie.'

Mr Burke pointed to the tie and boots on the floor. 'You can leave here whenever you want to. But stay with us for now. You're a grand worker.'

Eamonn's pride and anger had chewed away at his insides worse than any hunger. He had no strength left. He had no choice but to carry on working. The hope of saving up money and going to look for his mother and brothers was a thin, fragile thread, the only thing he could hold on to to stop himself falling into a deep, black hole.

THIRTEEN

The thin thread of hope was frayed and ready to break. Eamonn had almost given up waiting for news of his mother and brothers. When there was no reply to all his letters he asked the priest to see what he could find out, but there was still no news. Like his father's sister who had written them letters in Ireland urging them to leave everything and emigrate to America, his mother and brothers had vanished without a trace. Not killed by the great hunger in Ireland, not drowned on the voyage over, they had been lost, almost by accident, after all they had done to stay together. On that one afternoon when the good people of Quebec had come to Grosse Isle to choose their orphans to look after, Eamonn had taken his eyes off his brothers for ten minutes, twenty minutes at the most, and he had lost them.

He knew a lot of people would say he should be happy with the life he had found in Boston. The Bradys were a good family to live with, and he had Annie, the little sister who had adopted him. They all had work and enough to eat and they'd even been looking at another place to live, with rooms at street level instead of in the basement. And in a few months' time, once the weather had improved for passages across the Atlantic, Kate and her family, the best friends he had ever had in Ireland, would be joining them.

But it wasn't a crime to want to know what had happened to his own people. There were days when he felt as if a part of his mind had been ripped out, when he thought of the promise he had made to his father, to look after Mammy and the two boys. And he had looked after them, made them keep their courage up and not give in in spite of the dangers and the sickness at sea. And he had looked after them all the time they had been on Grosse Isle. And he'd only left the boys for ten minutes to see how his mother was, alone in her hospital ward.

Over and over again, he retraced his steps. In his mind he shouted louder than he had ever done at the doctor and at Mr Buchanan, pleading with them to let him stay with his mother, insisting that they tell him where they had taken his brothers. How could they have done that to his family? How could they have torn three brothers apart and made them leave their mother for dead? And Eamonn remembered the sermons he had sat through when the Buchanans took him to church on a Sunday, the way the priest praised the families who had taken in an Irish orphan. How many of them had taken in one good-looking little boy like Shaun and left the older brothers behind?

The whole of Boston was red and green and bright with snow for Christmas. Mrs Brady put money in a tin over the fire for a Christmas feast and Eamonn and Joe took the little ones for long walks past the downtown butchers where huge turkeys hung out for sale, draped with ivy. In the weeks before Christmas, the factory was buzzing, all of them worked longer hours and earned a bit more money. They had enough to eat. Their life was noisy, fast and full of laughter. Eamonn was hardly ever alone.

Whenever he was alone, he came back again to the question he had asked after the fire at Greshams Mills. What was the point of it all? What was the point of keeping people alive, keeping them out of danger, trying to get work if they were just going to get thrown out of work again? What was the point of working and saving, of writing letters and waiting and hoping, when he never heard anything back from his mother and brothers? He had seen so much struggle and people dying that he knew whatever he had now in Boston couldn't last. He remembered being happy on Grosse Isle, relieved that he had brought his family safely across the sea. But that happiness hadn't lasted. He didn't want to let himself be happy, in case that, too, was taken away from him.

Then Annie went missing.

She had gone off to school, as usual, with the others. And as usual she had dawdled because she didn't like school. They never waited for her because they knew she would turn up eventually, most days just before the bell. On the one day she had missed the bell, the teachers had given her the stick and then made her stand at the back of the class all day. So she wasn't usually late, however much she dawdled. And she had never missed school altogether.

At first, the teachers stuck to their idea that Annie was lazy, that she had just decided not to come to school. They said she would turn up before the end of the day and then she would be in very big trouble. When she hadn't arrived by the end of the day, they told the Brady children she would be waiting for them when they got home and they'd better tell their father to give her a good spanking.

But she wasn't at home and none of the smaller ones knew what to do. They told the neighbour who was supposed to keep an eye on them, but she said that Annie was just playing tricks, just being naughty. So they waited and waited until Mr and Mrs Brady, and Eamonn and Joe got home. And because it was almost Christmas and the factory was working right into the night to finish the last orders before the feast, none of them got home until half-past eight.

Losing Annie hit Eamonn like someone punching him in the stomach. He was winded, gasping for breath. He knew the minute he heard she was gone that she wasn't just playing tricks. It was a freezing cold night, with snow beginning to fall again and the streets outside made icy by rain that had fallen during the day and then frozen. He knew they should have been out searching all day, from the minute she didn't turn up at school. But when he first realized what was happening, he sank into a chair, his legs quite unable to carry him. He didn't want to lose Annie as well.

Mrs Brady stayed at home with the littlest ones and only William, the oldest apart from Joe, went out with them, retracing the route they took to school, trying to remember where they had last seen Annie.

'What was she wearing?' Mrs Brady searched through the pile of coats and woolly hats behind the door.

'She had that red hat on—that stupid one that Eamonn found one day outside one of his banks and brought home for her.' William started to cry. 'I told her she looked like a dwarf in it. And that's when she stopped walking with us.'

'She never walked with you,' Joe said. 'It's not your fault.'

'But we should have looked after her.' William's face was dirty from crying and a whole day of worrying about where she was.

'She was the oldest,' Joe said. 'It was her job to look after you. She had no business going wandering off like that.'

'We won't bring her back by fighting about what she should have done.' Mr Brady took William's hand. 'Tell us where she went on the days when she didn't come right away to school with you.'

'She went by the river. She always went by the river.'

Pain and fear lunged at Eamonn's stomach again. He had stood by the river enough himself, the last few weeks. He had taken Annie down to the river to show her the ducks paddling in smaller and smaller holes in the ice. He had told her about the man who threw himself off into the icy waters, and she had made him tell her the story again. 'Tell me about the man who threw himself off the bridge, Eamonn.' She had grabbed at his arm and made him take her there on a Sunday when there was no work. 'Why did he do it, Eamonn?'

And Eamonn had told her that people did that sort of thing when life had got too much for them. 'It's a way out,' he heard himself saying, 'when they can't stand the worrying about something any more.' Then he had taken her hand and told her, 'But you've got nothing to worry about, Annie. We'll take care of you.'

That wasn't true. He had come to the river often enough without Annie. He had come and stared into the river, thinking about his mother and brothers. He had walked away from their house to the river on his own when he could no longer see the point in anything, when he had asked himself what was the point of working and saving. He could see now, he had come to the river like a coward, running away from the things he had to fight. He had thought about following the man who had jumped off the bridge and disappeared into the frozen waters. And he had been quite prepared to leave Annie behind, breaking his promise to take care of her.

He couldn't bear it if Annie had left him behind, his little sister.

They started to walk towards the centre of town.

'She knows the way up here,' Joe said. 'We've been bringing them all to look at the turkeys. Maybe she just decided to take a day off school and look in the shops for Christmas.'

As long as they kept moving, Eamonn didn't feel so bad. It wasn't the cold that bothered him, so much as the fear, the pain of the fear like a knife. They walked all around the streets of downtown Boston. Church bells were ringing, the pavements were empty, and the lights from the shops had long been put out but they knew they would see her if she was around. Everything was in suspense. The horses' hooves were muffled by the snow as if they were caught in a dream. They wanted to stop passers-by and ask them, 'Have you seen a little girl with blonde curls and a red pixie-hood?' But nobody walked on their side of the street or stopped long enough to be asked.

Carriages drove past, people flew past, as fast as the flying snow. In the square in front of the city hall, Eamonn closed his eyes and whirled himself round, making a wish that she would be there when he opened his eyes. Tears blinded him, but when they had cleared there was still no sign of Annie.

'She's probably inside somewhere,' Joe said. 'In someone's house, where they've decided to take care of her. No one would leave a child outside on a night like this.'

Mr Brady shook his head. 'Let's hope there's no one, man, woman, or child who has to sleep outside tonight. Because it's going to freeze over more than a body could survive.' He sighed and scratched his head and turned a full circle, just as Eamonn had done. 'We can't stay out all night ourselves. We'll need to get William home at least.' He had William on his shoulders now, hitching the child up at every street corner as he gradually fell asleep and slipped down, his hands heavy on his father's neck.

'I'm not going home.' Eamonn stood and dug his hands deep into his pockets, the tears streaming down his face and icicles building in his hair from the snow that had turned to water. 'I'm not going home without Annie.'

'We can't do anything more tonight.' Mr Brady hitched William up onto his shoulders again and walked over to Eamonn. 'Someone good-hearted will have taken her in. Joe's right. No one will have left a child outside on a night like this.' He started to walk, slowly, away from the square. 'Come on, Eamonn. We can all be out searching at first light tomorrow.'

'She might be very close to here,' Eamonn said. 'I said I'd look after her. She might be needing us right now.' Then he shouted after the Bradys, 'I'm not coming home without her.'

Once they had disappeared and the square was completely quiet, he looked around. He knew they had done everything they could. There were thousands of houses in Boston. All they had done so far was walk around a few empty streets. If they didn't find her tonight they would have to start the next day, knocking on every door in the city. But he wasn't going to let her disappear, even if that meant someone else was taking care of her really well. He wasn't going to let other people tell him not to worry and then just do nothing while she slowly faded out of his life.

He had been having dreams, about his mother mainly. He had dreamed that he was walking up a gentle slope and that his mother was just behind him. He turned and smiled at her and she smiled back and waved. And as she waved, she seemed to slow down and drop back a little further behind him. But she was still very close. In his dream, he had been convinced that if he just stopped and waited for a very short time, she would catch up quickly. So he had carried on walking and the slope had got steeper and he had had to walk more slowly, catching his breath. And he had turned round and his mother had been suddenly much further back and still she had smiled and waved at him. So he had carried on, thinking in his dream that it was best for him to get to the summit of the long, steep walk before he stopped and waited for her to catch up.

He never reached the summit before he woke up out of his dream. But while he still had a long walk ahead of him, he turned round again. And his mother had completely disappeared.

He wasn't going to let that happen to Annie. He wasn't going to go away and leave her. But how could he find her when he didn't know where to look?

There was only one place they hadn't searched. On the stretch of river near the university was the tree under which Eamonn had slept when he first arrived in Boston, when the weather had been warm enough to sleep outside and he had nowhere else to go. He had often taken Annie there and talked about the tramps who slept under the bridge and had given him bits of food.

When he got to the tree, a policeman was already there. He was talking to somebody on the ground. 'Get up. You can't stay here.'

Eamonn rushed over and pulled his own coat off. 'Annie, you stupid girl. Get up. You can't stay here.'

Annie didn't open her eyes. She wasn't dead. That was impossible. She was too young to die. But she didn't move.

Eamonn touched her cheek. It was warm.

'Get up, Annie. We have to go home. It's too cold to stay here.'

Annie still didn't open her eyes, but she started to talk, squeezing her eyes tight shut as if she never wanted to wake up.

'Leave me alone. I'm too tired. All I need is a blanket.'

Eamonn kept on shaking her. 'Get up, Annie. You'll freeze to death.'

'Leave me alone. I'm cold. Where's the blanket?'

She had taken her own coat off and wrapped it around her legs, but her feet had been jutting out. Eamonn desperately tried to warm them, but Annie still didn't open her eyes.

'Annie! Get up! You can't stay here!'

'Leave me alone! Get me a blanket. Nobody cares.'

Eamonn was furious. 'I care! Get up out of that! Get up and do as I say.'

Annie opened her eyes then and said, 'I'm not going to school, Eamonn. I'm never going to school.' And she closed her eyes again, falling fast asleep.

In the end, he picked her up and carried her. And at every street corner he put her down, letting her lean her head against him to rest and then picked her up and carried her again until they reached their street. The lights in every house were on, even though it was way past midnight. And in the Bradys' house a crowd of neighbours were standing around, making plans for the search they were going to do the next day as soon as it was light.

Eamonn, bringing home the dirty, sleepy little girl, was clapped and cheered and kissed more than he had ever been kissed in his life before and then Annie was tucked up in bed. But instead of falling into an even deeper sleep, she opened her eyes and asked for Eamonn.

'I'm never going to school again, Eamonn,' she said. 'Don't make me go to that school.'

The letter was not from Dermot. Not from the brother he knew.

'Read me your letter, Eamonn. Read it now!'

Annie sat on his knee, pointing to the words in round, neat handwriting. It wasn't Dermot, with writing like that.

The kitchen was quiet. They all knew how long he'd been waiting for news of his family. Smiling, excited eyes looked at each other, looked at Eamonn and then towards the letter from Dermot, his brother, willing him to read it out loud.

Eamonn looked down at a sea of blue words that swam and blurred in front of him. It wasn't his brother. It couldn't be his brother, Dermot, who started off a letter in neat, unrecognizable handwriting, 'Dearest Brother . . . '

The kettle on the hob started to splutter and whistle, and Mrs Brady moved it to one side while Eamonn read the words again, 'Dearest Brother . . . '

He shook his head. 'That's not Dermot.' He held up the letter. 'That's not the way he writes.'

Annie grabbed the letter from him.

' 'Course it's Dermot, you great nincompoop!'

She sat and traced the first two words with her

finger. ' "Dearest Brother . . . " What's he writing a thing like that for if he's not your brother?'

'But he can't write as well as that. He never had as much school as I did back home.'

'Well maybe he's been at school all this time.'

Eamonn read out the address at the top of the letter. It was a boarding school north of Quebec.

'A Jesuit school, it'll be.' Mr Brady was as proud as if he was talking about his own son. 'A very good school. It's the Jesuits have taught him how to be refined, I'll bet you.'

'Just read me the letter, Eamonn.' Annie scored under the lines of writing with her finger. 'Read me the letter and I'll tell you if it's your brother or not.' She brushed her curls out of the way where they were hanging over the letter. 'He's my brother too, you know. I ought to know if it's from him or not.'

So Eamonn read the letter out to them.

'Dearest Brother, I am writing to tell you that I am very happy here in Canada with my new family. I hope you are happy too, with the good people who took you away from the island. Dr and Mrs Scott, with whom I am to live during my school holidays . . . '

'With whom I am to live!' Annie wrinkled up her nose and laughed. 'Lord, doesn't he just talk!'

'Sounds very nice and proper.' Mrs Brady stood and looked over Eamonn's shoulder at the paper she couldn't read.

'Go on, Eamonn, read us some more.' Mr Brady leaned against the side of the hearth and shifted the guard.

Eamonn read on quickly and then summed the letter up. The letter from Dermot said he was doing really well at school. The family who had adopted him had sent him away to a Jesuit school for boys and told him they only wanted to hear about him doing well, so he had worked very hard from the minute he arrived there and now he was always top of his class. 'They've got four daughters, his family. And they live in a big house with servants. And all of them with their own rooms. And Dermot wishes me well and sends his love to Shaun and our mother.' Eamonn turned the letter over, so no one could read it. 'Sends his love to our mother. He's even forgotten that we call her Mammy.'

'Does even Dermot have his own room, Eamonn?' Annie clung round the back of his neck and hung there as he tried to stand up. 'Show me the bit about the rooms, Eamonn.' But Mr Brady took the little girl up and set her down on the floor.

'Hush now, Annie. Leave him be.'

They watched Eamonn, the whole kitchen still quiet, wanting to make the news in the letter better than it was.

Dermot had never received any of the letters Eamonn had written to him. The Jesuit Fathers had made sure that only the letters from his new family got through— because they said it was best for him to turn his back on his old family. So the first letter Eamonn received from his brother had been smuggled out by another boy going home for the holidays. It came from a brother he hardly knew, a boy who was holy and hard-working and said it was a sin to be ungrateful to the Scotts who had taken him away from his family and then sent him off to be educated by the Jesuits. At least Eamonn knew that one of his brothers was still alive and well. But there was still no news of their mother. And Shaun had vanished without a trace.

Eamonn sat and thought for a long time, trying to work out what would be the right thing to do. He let Joe look at the letter and then Mr and Mrs Brady. 'He's doing all right there,' Mrs Brady said. 'He'll probably make a grand life for himself, with the good education they're giving him.'

'But he's got no real family,' Mr Brady said. 'What sort of a life is that?'

Eamonn was uneasy. The boy in the letter wasn't like his brother. He wasn't even sure he liked him any longer. But he knew he should be pleased that his brother had got himself a better place, with the chance of getting a good education. Perhaps he was just jealous of his brother's life. He had always wanted them to go to school and learn something useful. That was what their father had wanted for them. Now at least Dermot was going to learn a lot. The only thing Eamonn was learning was the work he did every day from six in the morning.

'Dermot might even decide to become a priest,' Mrs Brady said. 'And wouldn't your mother be proud of him then?'

'But she wouldn't have wanted him to be all alone with the Jesuits, far away from us when he's only twelve.' Eamonn saw Dermot as he had been the last day on Grosse Isle, thin and pale and cold.

'Would you want that?' Mr Brady patted his wife's hair. 'You wouldn't want any of this lot to go away, even if they did get to be a priest in the end. It's not natural to send them away, like that. I think Eamonn ought to go and get him, so he can come and live with us.'

Mrs Brady held out both her hands, pointing out the size of their rented rooms and the size of the family they already had. Then she shrugged her shoulders and grinned. 'If you can work miracles, we can feed the five thousand.'

'At least go and ask the poor laddie what he really wants. At least give him the chance to say, "I want to stay with the Jesuits in this posh school," or,' and Mr Brady laughed as if he had just made up the best joke ever, ' "I want to go and live in a very small cellar in Boston with a very large family." '

'I know what I would say, Eamonn.' Annie flung her arms around his neck and sat on his knee again, waiting for him to pick her up and carry her around the very small room.

'And what would you say?'

'I'd say, "Take me away from this rotten old school and let me stay home with the Bradys."'

'But you're not my brother.'

Mr Brady went to Kate's father with the story, just as he did if any one of the other workers needed help. And Kate's father heard for the first time how hard Eamonn had tried to save money to get his family back together again and how he never earned enough and couldn't save as fast as the prices were going up for travelling by train.

'There's no harm in looking at work in Canada,' he said. 'We could maybe get to do business up there.' And he fixed up for Eamonn to travel up north as a messenger boy with the men he always sent out to get new business. For six weeks he would have time to visit all the places he had last heard of them, to look for his mother and brothers and bring them back, if Boston was where they wanted to stay.

'He's the best,' Mrs Brady said back home in their kitchen that night. 'We couldn't wish for a better boss.'

'He's all right as far as bosses go,' Mr Brady said. 'But he's no saint. He could do more.'

'What more could he do? You talk rot, Michael Brady, you really do. He's the kindest best man we ever saw.'

Annie stepped between them to stop them doing what they never had done before, having a grand old row. But Mr Brady carried on.

'It's not good enough being kind. Someone else could buy his factory from him tomorrow and unless they were just as kind as him, we'd be back where we started.'

FOURTEEN

The Jesuit Fathers had told Dermot it was a sin to think about his old family now that he had a new father paying for his education and a new family who loved him. The Fathers drilled it into him, and to seven other boys at the school who had been adopted since they came to America. Having a new family meant they were morally bound to forget the old.

So Dermot was afraid of meeting his brother. And he knew he would never tell, not even in confession where he was bound to tell all his sins, that he had arranged to meet Eamonn, at the railway station in Quebec, in the hour he had to wait for Dr Scott to meet him. It was raining. Dermot was afraid. He scanned the almost empty platform, not wanting to let his eyes rest on the one boy in the station, the small, pale boy who reminded him of Eamonn, but couldn't possibly be his older brother.

Dermot had grown taller and Eamonn had stayed the same height, in all the time they had been separated. Dermot had had a quiet life, working hard at school, while Eamonn had had to struggle to stay alive. But Eamonn recognized Dermot, even in his strange, smart uniform, sitting on the huge trunk the Scotts had bought for him. He walked slowly along the platform, his cap in his hand and rainwater dripping from his hair and then stopped in front of his brother.

'They must be giving you enough food.' Eamonn stood well back and grinned at his brother, standing under the shelter of the platform canopy. 'Three meals a day?'

Dermot spoke differently and Eamonn's question seemed strange to him now. Once you had enough to eat, you didn't think about food any longer. Oh, he had thought about it often enough when he was first separated from his brothers. That had been his only thought when he first arrived at his boarding school and was left alone in the long, narrow dormitory. Whether his brothers were getting enough to eat. But Eamonn's question was part of a life Dermot had already put behind him. Nobody at the Scotts' house ever talked about food. And if they talked about people not getting enough to eat, it was the poor, black babies in Africa, their thin, sad faces pictured on the collection boxes every Sunday.

In his thoughts and in his dreams, Eamonn had pictured himself meeting with Dermot almost every day. He had seen how they both rushed into each other's arms and laughed and cried and hugged each other. Every day he had tried to grasp the delight of that first meeting before the images faded, but he had never kept hold of it. Now he had Dermot in front of him, he didn't know what to feel. He didn't know what to say. His arms refused to reach out and clasp the stranger in front of him and Dermot didn't make any move to even shake his hand. Eamonn wanted to let go of his self-control and cry out loud, wail and cry like a disappointed toddler, as he struggled to find words to say to the brother he hardly knew.

Eamonn got Dermot to sit down on the green bench under the canopy and told him about his job. 'I'm a messenger boy. You should see the banks and the grand shops. You'd like to see Boston, I know you would, Dermot.' He had enough money for a ticket home with Dermot, but he didn't dare to ask him to leave everything behind and come back to Boston. Dermot was a different person, with a different life. When he knew he should have been thinking of his brother and the joy of finding him again, all he could think of was what the others would make of him, back in Boston, this boy with a strange accent and the way he had of talking like a priest?

'We don't have much time before my father, Dr Scott, arrives.' Dermot wore a watch on a chain and he pulled it out of the pocket of his grey waistcoat. 'Less than an hour, I'm afraid.'

They didn't talk about Ireland or about their little brother, Shaun. Neither of them wanted to ask the questions that might bring bad news. That was why both brothers kept until last the question they most wanted to ask.

'Have you heard from Mammy?'

And when Eamonn said he was heading out to Grosse Isle to see what he could find out about her, Dermot said, 'Give her my love,' and they promised to write to each other.

Then Eamonn hid behind a pillar on the platform and watched as Dermot shook hands with a tall man in a brown, tweed suit who helped him lift his trunk onto a porter's wagon. Eamonn's face froze into a mask as he stopped himself from calling out, pleading with Dermot not to leave him again. It was wrong for his brother to have to walk away like that and ignore him. And yet it was good for Dermot to be living where he was. Eamonn fought with himself, wanting to run after them and call Dermot back and then telling himself he was just jealous because now it was Dermot going to school. He stayed rooted to the spot, clinging to one of the green-painted pillars that held up the canopy over the platform.

'You have to let him go.' He spat the words out, staring down at the glistening, wet cobblestones. Then he stepped out from under the canopy, lifting his head up towards the sky so the freezing rain could bathe his eyes. They were stinging and burning and he was blinded, the pain like a jet of acid hurled into his face.

'He'll have a grand life. You have to let him go. Let go.'

He shook his head and pressed his fists over his open eyes. Then he strode quickly towards the entrance to the platform. He wasn't going to cry. Nobody was going to see Eamonn Kennedy crying.

What Eamonn remembered of Grosse Isle was the mass of ships just offshore waiting to disembark their cargoes of people. He remembered the rows of army tents as far as the eye could see and the echoing noises of children shouting out to each other, playing tag among the tent ropes, mingled with the sounds of people crying out in their fever. He remembered the smell of the sea and the smell of death and sickness that had hung over the place whenever you couldn't get right to the edge of the cliffs to breathe freely. He remembered the crashing of waves and the trickling and splashing of the narrow pipes that came up above ground just beyond their row of tents and carried their stinking load into the sea. He remembered the mounds of newly dug graves and the places where the men had had to try and dig the graves again because they hadn't been able to dig deep enough into the already frozen October earth. And he remembered Dr Douglas, exhausted, never stopping, with the small band of workers he had for the whole of the island and the never ending stream of ships beyond.

Eamonn remembered the hospital too. In his sleep, he could have walked from the jetty where he had disembarked to leave the island back to the hospital, through the entrance hall, along the sparkling green floor of the long corridors and through the long line of wards that led to the ward where he had last seen his mother, at the far end under the tall window. He made the journey to the bed at the end of the ward in his thoughts all the time he was journeying up north to Quebec to see Dermot and all the time he was travelling on towards Grosse Isle. By the time he reached the island and got to the hospital, he had made the journey in his thoughts so often that he already knew what he was going to find at the end of it. He stood in Dr Douglas's office and the old man looked up, surprised, and shook his hand and said, 'No one has ever come back to see me, laddie. No one has ever wanted to come back here when once they've left.'

By the time Eamonn held the doctor's hand and looked into his eyes, he knew that his mother had died the day he left the island. How could he have believed anything else? Had he really believed that Mammy, if she were alive, would have ignored all his letters, would not have moved heaven and earth to get them all back together again? He realized that the very idea of her, the idea of what she would say if she knew he was on the point of giving up, was what had kept him going. If he had had to accept then, right at the beginning of his life in America, that he was completely alone, he wouldn't have had the strength to carry on.

It was well over a year since they had arrived on the island. Only half as many immigrants had arrived that second year and there was less work for Dr Douglas to do, though still enough to keep him occupied for the whole day. In the evening, he walked with Eamonn through the hospital. The ward where he had last seen his mother was, at the start of the shipping season, completely empty, and they stood underneath the long, narrow window, looking down towards the cliffs and the sea.

'I am sorry your mother had to die here,' the doctor said. 'There were very few survived. The fever was merciless.'

Eamonn closed his eyes, trying to shut out the sunset over the sea and the stinging pain that was taking him over against his will. He was in control. He had to remain in control. He wasn't a child any longer. There was Annie to look after. He had to look for Shaun. There was his job and the long journey back to Boston. He couldn't afford to lose control. And besides, he shouldn't blame the doctor. More than anyone else, he had done his best and worked day and night to save people.

The tears Eamonn was holding back squeezed themselves into a suffocating, burning smoke, swirling round his head and numbing him. He turned and strode away towards the door, into the shadows, so the doctor wouldn't see him gasping for air, his face gasping for control. Then, from the far end of the ward he lost control of the grown man he was trying to be and turned and shouted at the doctor who stood with his back towards him, looking out of the window.

'You couldn't save my mother. But you didn't have to take my brothers away as well! Why did you take my brothers away?'

The doctor turned to face him, but still the whole of him was in shadow, the bright glow of the setting sun behind him.

'I had to take care of the living as well as the dying. And the only way I could see of taking care of all you children was to let those good people adopt you. Did they not treat you well? Did they not give you enough to eat?'

'I could have managed with less to eat! We managed with not much to eat for years. But why did you take away my brothers?'

The bed springs creaked as the doctor sat down on the mattress of the bed nearest the window. 'It wasn't right, Eamonn. I know it wasn't right. But we couldn't ask those good people to take more than one child, to take three or four. And besides, there weren't enough children to go round. The day you left, there were sixty families came here, all wanting to do their Christian duty, all wanting to take a child off my hands. And we only had fifty children.'

'You took away my brothers.'

Eamonn grew cold with the shock he hadn't allowed himself to feel that afternoon when he arrived back in the doctors' quarters and found he was the only one still left behind. He was suddenly very tired, shaking, his arms and legs hollow. He too sat down.

'And why did you never tell me what had happened? I wrote you letters, asking about my brothers. Why did you never write to me?'

The doctor's voice came faintly across the room like a bright light being cut right back by a heavy mist. Eamonn thought there must be something wrong with his ears, but he heard the words, 'I only received your letters last month, when we opened this place again. And the bishop thought it was best for all of you if you didn't make contact with people from your past life. He said that would make you unhappy with your new families.'

There was a long silence. None of the anger was any use. The people Eamonn needed to be angry with were far away. Still sitting, he put his head down on the hard, harsh mattress. He heard the bedsprings echoing his breathing. He had come to the end of his journey and he only wanted to sleep. The doctor spoke again, gently, his voice carrying Eamonn into sleep.

'You weren't the only one who ran away, you know. There were others who refused to stay with their new families.' Eamonn was almost asleep, but he heard the doctor saying, 'The children who ran away are in orphanages in Quebec. Maybe you'll find your little brother, Shaun, if he hasn't been adopted since. His family put him there, I know, because he bit and kicked and scratched them all and ran away whenever he could. Like a wild animal, they said he was, when he found out you weren't going to be with him. The last thing I heard, he screamed at the bishop, "I don't want a new life. I don't want a new family. I want my brothers."'

The doctor was obviously amused by the way nobody had been able to make Shaun do what he didn't want to do. Eamonn fell asleep thinking of the Shaun he had last seen, the good little boy with flame-red hair and freckles who did whatever he was told.

With the address of the orphanage in Quebec, Eamonn had nothing more to keep him on the island. But the doctor took him to the cemetery, in the valley beneath Telegraph Hill. None of the graves were marked. Most of the people buried there would remain nameless. There had been too many of them to care for in life and no one to care for them when they were dead. So the doctor had decided to collect money and build a monument. He showed Eamonn the drawings of what was going to be built and the words they were going to carve on the stone. On one side they were going to have the names of doctors who had died—doctors Eamonn had never met because the last one had died in August before their ship had docked. On the other side there would be an inscription for people like Eamonn's mother, whose grave had no name. In beautiful, italic handwriting on the design for the monument, they had written:

'In this secluded spot lie the mortal remains of 5,424 persons who, flying from Pestilence and Famine in Ireland in the year 1847, found in America but a grave.'

So many people dying. It didn't make sense. Eamonn remembered the rows of army tents, the rows of hospital beds, the ships crowded out at anchor, but he had never begun to count the people on the island in the months that they lived there. He remembered the people dying on the ship they had taken from Liverpool, even the captain and the wealthiest passengers. But more than five thousand people dying didn't make sense. He had seen how the doctor had worked. Other doctors had given their lives. It didn't make sense that nothing could be done, that nothing had been done while more than five thousand people died.

He never saw the doctor again and never went back to the island, though he promised the doctor he would, to see the monument when it was finally built. They had to move on, to the life he was starting to build further to the south.

All the boys in the orphanage looked the same. At least they looked the same at first, in grey jerseys and short breeches, with thick, black wool socks and stout black boots. Eamonn stood in the entrance hall and pressed his face to the glass window that looked down into the assembly hall below. A hundred little boys stood with heads bowed while prayers were said, a hundred little boys with the same dark clothing and polished boots and hands folded in prayer. Except that one little boy, one out of the whole assembled group, had his hands behind his back, not folded in prayer but clenched into fists.

Eamonn looked up and down the rows. All the others had hands joined at the front, heads bowed. The little boy with his hands twisted behind his back, clenched into upturned fists, stood out among the crowd. Eamonn glanced behind him to see if anyone else had picked out the little boy from the vantage point of the window above the hall. But there was no one else around. The Brother in charge of the door had told Eamonn to wait for the end of prayers because all the teachers and Brothers were down in the body of the hall. Eamonn found himself pressing his fists behind him as he pressed his face against the glass, hoping that no one would notice the little boy, wanting to save him from the trouble he was bound to get himself into if he kept on being different to all the others.

It was Shaun. He had grown taller and his face was longer now, not the round, cherub face that had made him be one of the first to be taken off the island. He looked tougher too, not like a baby brother any more. But it was Shaun. When they gave out hymn books, he looked up and recognized Eamonn from down below in the hall. Like a rabbit let out of a trap he surged forwards, pushing his way along his row to get out of the hall as fast as he could. Two of the Brothers, in their long black robes and square white collars, flapped and tried to catch Shaun as he made his way past the other astonished boys, ignoring the Brother Superior shouting orders from the stage. But he slipped through their hands, disappeared for a moment and then ran up the stairs and threw himself on Eamonn.

'I knew you were coming. I knew you were coming.' He swung himself round and jumped up into Eamonn's arms as he always used to do when he was small enough to be carried around all day. He laughed out loud and turned and smiled at the Brother Superior who had made it to the top of the stairs. 'They said you would have forgotten all about me by now, Eamonn. And they said I had to forget you. But I knew you were coming. They just didn't believe me.' He grinned at the Brother Superior and clung to Eamonn, his arms like the chains around a treasure chest.

Then he wanted to go and get Dermot. 'Why hasn't Dermot come with you? Haven't you got him yet?'

Eamonn tried to explain the way Dermot had changed. He talked about the cellar in Boston where he lived in the three rooms with the Brady family and about the good school Dermot was going to, with his three good meals a day.

'We can't take him away from a good school, Shaun. He's doing really well.'

'Did you ask him, our Eamonn? Did you ask him what he wants?'

'I didn't need to ask him. He says he's doing well. He's going to get a good education. That's all a man needs if he's going to go far in the world. That's what Daddy used to say.'

'He needs his brothers most.'

Eamonn looked up. He had been watching Shaun, stuffing his possessions, a stone he had picked up when they left their village, a farthing someone had given him while they were still in Liverpool, a pair of pyjamas, into a canvas bag. One of the Brothers carried on talking as Shaun packed the bag they had given him with the few pieces of clothing he had left on his shelf in the dormitory.

The Brother sat down beside Shaun and patted him on the head. 'I'm glad you've come to get him,' he said. 'He's a grand little lad, though some people here said he had the devil in him. He was only missing his brothers. It's only natural. And if you've another brother he'll be missing you an' all.'

Eamonn shrugged his shoulders. 'We can ask him,' he said, 'if he's still in Quebec.'

He knew the address of the house where Dermot stayed during the holidays with the Scott family.

The house was large and long and elegant, with seven tall windows upstairs and six windows and a shiny black door downstairs. A narrow path led through lawns and flower beds. It was Shaun who rang the bell when Eamonn lost his nerve. 'I want to see my brother,' he whispered, jumping up behind Eamonn as he hesitated. 'Where's the harm in that?'

A maidservant answered the door, a thin young girl who inspected the empty path behind them to see if they had brought any other poor-looking individuals with them and then said, 'Dr Scott isn't at home today.'

'We've come to see Dermot.' Shaun grinned.

'I'll have to tell my mistress. Whom shall I say is calling?'

The girl had only just learned the words to use when she opened the door, because she had only started working with them the day before. Eamonn grinned as well. 'Just tell them please that Eamonn's here.'

'Whom?' The girl's eyebrows rose and she looked ready to drop the posh way she had been taught to speak and tell them to stop fooling around.

'Just Eamonn.'

Dermot came into the hall before she had a chance to go and get her mistress or make the formal announcements she had practised the day before. And this time he was the brother Eamonn remembered. Shaun flew into his arms and Dermot yelled, 'I thought you'd never come back. I thought I'd never see you again.' And they all sat down together on the floor, with their arms around each other and cried.

They cried for their mother and the days and months of time they'd lost. They cried because they'd found each other. Eamonn cried without thinking, without noticing he was crying after years of rationing every tear.

The servant girl had run off and came back with Mrs Scott and her four daughters, the cook, and the gardener. And all of them stood in a circle round the three brothers, clapping and laughing like the audience at a play. Then Shaun jumped up and ran round the two brothers still on the floor, pulling at their hair as they sat and grinned at each other and punching them in the back and shouting out, 'I knew they were coming for me. I knew it. But no one believed me.' Then he went round and kissed each of the sisters, Mrs Scott, and the cook.

'Say something, Eamonn.'

Dermot sat and looked at his brother. And grinned.

'You're not going to go away again, are you?'

'I'm not going to lose you, now that I've found you both.'

They stayed for three days with Dermot's new family. Doctor Scott swore more than a good doctor should and swore even more, on the second day of their visit, when he realized how he had been deceived the day they had gone to Grosse Isle and driven home with Dermot.

'They told me all of his family were dead.' He stood by the fire and put his arm around Eamonn's shoulder. 'They said that Dermot refused to admit that his family were dead and I had to make him face up to it.' He looked round for Shaun, but Shaun was being spoiled, out in the garden on the swing, with all four sisters taking turns to push him.

'I would have taken all three of you if only I had known.'

'They can stay with us now. Why not?'

Mrs Scott closed the door of the living room behind her and went over to the high window that looked out over the huge lawn with its tall trees and the swing. From the far end of the garden they could still hear Shaun squealing with delight, the first time he had ever been on a swing.

'You will stay with us, Eamonn, won't you?' Mrs Scott sat down on one of the long, flowered settles under the window. Eamonn sat down on the opposite side of the room, with Dermot. The room was warmed by a blanket of stillness, ruffled only by the ticking clock and the gentle creak of the tree with the swing. The four sisters had finally sat down, leaving Shaun to practise swinging himself to and fro, to and fro, backwards and forwards, backwards and forwards.

Irish and American, Canada and Boston, Quebec and Boston, Quebec and Liverpool, Galway and Tullamore, American and Irish, backwards and forwards, backwards and forwards, to and fro, to and fro. The old tree creaked from the gentle breeze and the swing going backwards and forwards, Shaun swinging higher and higher. The Scotts wanted only the best for Eamonn and his brothers. Wanted to anchor them to this one beautiful house on the edge of Quebec, to make them feel they belonged somewhere. But it was too late for that. They were strangers everywhere now, always passing through on their journey to somewhere else. Ever since they had been thrown out of their turf house in Ballinglas by the British soldiers they had lived as strangers. But that didn't mean they couldn't be happy, as Shaun was now, whooping with joy as he managed to stand up on the seat of the swing and keep his balance. And that didn't mean they couldn't be happy as Eamonn was now, quietly watching his little brother's happiness, proud of the schoolwork Dermot had shown him.

They talked and talked for hours about the schools the brothers could go to and which rooms they should have if they stayed with the Scotts, but Eamonn couldn't rest. He had a second family now and ties he didn't want to break. The year they had been separated had made him part of the Brady family, with Annie to look after and a good job to do for Kate's father. He was sure now that he wouldn't lose touch with Dermot and he could see that Dermot was safe and well. He struggled with what was best for his brothers. He tried, whenever they were left alone, to persuade Shaun that it would be much better for him to stay and live with the Scotts and get himself sent to the same school as Dermot. But Shaun wouldn't change his mind about leaving Eamonn.

'We can come and see Dermot every summer,' he said. 'I want to stay with you.'

Eamonn knew it was right not to encourage Dermot to join them in Boston. Dermot had the chance to do really well for himself. It would be madness to give up a good school and a kind family and move to work in a factory and live in a crowded basement in Boston. Dermot could write to them now, whenever he wanted. That was all that mattered. Eamonn had lost his brothers, given them up for dead. Now they were alive and nothing else mattered.

That evening, Eamonn walked around the Scotts' large garden, his head fit to burst with excitement and happiness. At the end of the garden, out of sight of the house and under a large fir tree, he flung himself down on the hard, damp ground and opened and closed his eyes, opened and closed them, looking out at the flying grey clouds and the beginnings of a sunset and then looking into his store of memories, of everything that had happened to them.

He saw himself on the hill where the monument was going to be to the 5,424 people who had fled from Ireland and then died on Grosse Isle. He saw himself in the room where he had last seen his mother. He saw his tearful, desperate self searching through freezing Boston for Annie, and his desperation when they lost their jobs and he knew he wouldn't be able to go searching for his brothers.

'Red sky at night is the shepherd's delight.'

The whole of the sky was orange and pink and purple. Someone was calling Eamonn into the house, from a long way away. There was dinner on the table. There were warm beds to sleep in, soft beds in large clean rooms at the Scotts' house. There were beds shared with other children in the basement in Boston, but still there were beds to sleep in and enough to eat.

And in another week, by the time he was back in Boston, Kate should be arriving from Ireland, with Peter and little Joe and her stepmother.

Eamonn squeezed his eyes shut.

Thousands of miles from home, battered and alone, after everything was lost, he felt he had come home again. He and his brothers would do something good with their lives in America. He was sure of that. They had travelled too far to sit back and watch people chained and dragged down by hunger, and sickness, and desperation.

His eyes were open again, and he stared up at the sky. He knew now why he had lost his brothers and then found them again. He knew now where he and his brothers were going. He knew that he would do everything in his power to make sure that the hunger and sickness that had nearly wiped out his whole family never happened to anyone else.

Also by Elizabeth Lutzeier

The Coldest Winter
ISBN 0 19 275202 2

'For pity's sake!' shouted Eamonn's father. 'The man's got five children. Leave him a roof over his head.'

But the English soldiers either couldn't understand Irish, or else someone had put a spell on them, freezing their hearts so that they couldn't feel any pity for the children who were going to have to sleep out in the cold fields.

It is 1846 in Ireland and the potato harvest has failed. When Eamonn and his father had started digging, the potato plants were all green, and a soft gentle rain had cleared the air. But overnight the potato blight poisoned everything and their food for the whole year had rotted.

English soldiers turned families out of their homes, the roads were full of people with nowhere to go, and there was no work. Ireland was no place for the living—not unless you had a lot of money and a big warm house.

This is the story of how Eamonn and his family tried to stay alive in spite of the cold and famine, and how with the help of a young girl, Kate Burke, they tried to survive through the coldest winter Ireland had ever known.

Crying for the Enemy
ISBN 0 19 275258 8

One Monday morning in April 1916, the day after Easter, a boy and two girls set out from different places, each on their own separate journey to the centre of Dublin. They had no idea how their journeys would end.

Easter Monday, 1916, one of the most momentous and terrible days in the troubled history of Ireland, when a group of rebels try to wrest the government of their country from the might of the British Empire. Michael is determined to play his part in the historic events. His brother may be fighting for the British in the trenches of Flanders, but Michael will fight for his country's freedom—to the death, if necessary. Daisy is American, but her parents are Irish, and she is prepared to do anything for the cause—and girls can fight as well as men, for what they believe in.

Sarah just wants to be a nurse, to do her bit to help the wounded soldiers back from the battlefields in France, soldiers like her brother. But when the hospital in Dublin Castle gets caught in the uprising, Sarah finds her loyalties stretched to the limit. How can Irishmen be her enemy? She just wants to see an end to the killing, an end to the fear.